THE WARRIOR OWL

Verses Kindler Publication

VERSES KINDLER PUBLICATION

Verses Kindler Publication.

Website: www.verseskindlerpublication.com

© Copyright, 2024, Mr. Yogesh Nair

The Warrior Owl
By: Mr. Yogesh Nair
ISBN: 978-93-5605-770-8

NON-FICTION STORIES 1st Edition
Price: INR 300/ $15

Disclaimer

The Warrior Owl is written by Yogesh Nair.

The published work is the original contents of the author and he has done his best to edit and make it plagiarism-free.

The characters may be fictitious or based on real events but they are not meant to hurt anyone's feelings nor portray anything against any caste or system. Any resemblance of names of actual person, place or institute is purely coincidental to carry forward the story.

In case of any plagiarized write-up, the author is solely responsible for it, the publisher would not be responsible for it.

Dedication

To the brave soldiers of the Indian Army, whose courage and sacrifice deserve every honor.

To my father, Late Shri Gopalkrishna Nair, whose blessings from heaven guide me and keep me steadfast in my journey.

To the four incredible women who are my world: My mother, Vijaya Nair, whose love and wisdom shape my life; my wife, Shalini, whose support and partnership are my greatest strengths; and my daughters, Aastha and Aanchal, whose joy and spirit light up my days.

And to my friends and colleagues, whose persistent support and camaraderie are a source of strength in the toughest of times.

This book is a testament to all of you.

Acknowledgments

Dear reader, thank you for taking the time to immerse yourself in these pages. Your willingness to engage with my work and share in the journey of this book means more to me than words can express.

It is my deepest hope that this book brings you as much joy, insight, and inspiration as it has brought me in the process of creating it. Your support and enthusiasm are the greatest rewards, and for that, I am truly grateful.

Table of Contents

Chapter 1: The Bird of The Night Rises

On a moonlit night in a remote forest in Melghat, a peaceful silence had settled over. It was the epitome of tranquillity and the only noise falling on one's ears was the soft whoosh of the birds awakened at night or the chirps of crickets. A woman, who had come to be idolized within the locality as the pinnacle of strength and resilience, trudged wearily toward the doorstep of her home and her eyes took in the calming vista that had the perfect symphony of silhouettes of trees and the glow of the moon and stars. Sridevi deeply breathed in the crisp and pure air, soaked the peaceful silence, and moments later emitted a loud scream that shattered the stillness.

She was preparing herself for the most transformational experience of her life. The birth of her baby was imminent, and a series of unavoidable circumstances had led to her husband being away for this momentous occasion. The feeling of being alone and single-handedly managing things at such critical times is not something that is ordinarily easy to cope with. However, this was no ordinary woman either. Sridevi had the spirit of a fighter and enormous courage flowing through her veins. She screamed out loud once again; it was not a cry of agony or despair but rather a fierce cry to steel herself to rise to the occasion and do what needed to be done. They had not been expecting the baby for another few days, and hence it had not crossed their minds to prepare for such an eventuality. Sridevi smiled at her womb and lovingly said to it, "We've started troubling Maa right from the beginning, have we?" Her question was answered with a series of vigorous kicks, and she knew she needed to act soon.

Their house was in a private and secluded area, and while they usually enjoyed the solitude, it presented an additional complication for Sridevi. She knew no decibel of sound that she produced would reach anyone's ears; she started slowly inching forward, staggering and stumbling with each step. The walk was just a few minutes long, but it felt like she had been at it for hours.

Eventually, she spotted a man who could help her and loudly yelled out to him to wait. Before he could comprehend the scene unfolding in front of his eyes, Sridevi had made her way toward him and hauled herself into his bullock cart. He was terrified looking at her condition; he had the greatest regard for her and her husband, and the idea of letting them down for the most significant moment of their lives had scared the man. Sridevi was enduring pain of an unfathomable magnitude, but even through that, she was reassuring him to not panic and comforting him that he would get them to the hospital in time.

He came through for her, and shortly after reaching the hospital, she delivered a beautiful and healthy baby boy.

Every baby cries upon birth, but there was something that set him apart. A newborn's wail generally showcases discomfort, urgency & frailty. But when this particular baby cried, he embodied his mother and displayed no signs of weakness or vulnerability. It was a loud, assertive, and self-assured wail with rhythmic bursts; it resonated throughout the hospital, and everyone who heard it marveled at the fact that a small newborn could generate such a powerful sound.

This was the earliest indication of the child growing up to be a magnetic personality who commanded attention and respect from everyone he met, and never slowed down even in the face of difficulties.

The hospital staff used to bicker with each other to get a posting for the care of this child, for they were completely fascinated with him. While other babies could barely support their own heads at such an age, this one used to be frantically moving his limbs and eagerly looking around. It was a frequent joke among all his visitors that he had global-level affairs to attend to and hence did not want to waste his time lying in the cot. They also noticed that whenever he wished to not be parted from his mother, he showed unwavering resolve and used every bit of his strength to grip onto her. They could see his tiny hands digging into his mother's skin in an attempt to hold on. Sridevi always gave in, and the hospital staff laughingly told her that she had given birth to a headstrong ox.

It was an irrefutable fact that this baby was meant for great things and that he personified determination, grit, and tenacity. And through the course of his glorious life, that is exactly what Advay Varma achieved.

Sridevi and her husband, Anand, were fairly new to their environment and yet they had taken to it like a fish to water. As a forest officer, Anand's time was largely devoted to the demands of his job. He was required to visit numerous forest outposts for inspections and checks, and he was the most hardworking, passionate, and meticulous official that the forests had ever been blessed with. For Sridevi, the cultural and lifestyle difference between their current home and the previous one in Kerala had initially been a lot to cope with. However, she had finely risen to the occasion and immersed herself in learning and acclimating to the ways of the people there and helping them in whatever ways she could. In between all these, the new parents had not found a quiet moment for a discussion on what their child should be named. But that decision had to be made soon, and it was not one that could be lightly made.

Many people offered many suggestions to the new parents, but none of them felt right. Sridevi looked at her baby who was curiously taking in all the new sights around him, and determinedly kicking off the blanket that the nurse kept trying to put over his legs. She smiled fondly and a name that she had heard a long time ago popped into her mind. She knew Advay would be the most befitting name for her child, for it signified uniqueness and the possession of qualities like none other.

Sridevi and Anand were very well-liked within the village and town, and almost all the inhabitants from there flocked in to see their child and bless him. They were astonished to see his attractive features, for it was unlike anything they had seen before. He had adorably chubby cheeks, large eyes with a delicate nose, and a mischievous smile that was highly endearing. He seldom cried and spent most of his time trying to make sense of the new world that he found himself in. He was also notorious for keeping his mother awake with him all through the night.

The hospital staff started affectionately calling him 'owl' due to his liking for staying up during the night-time and his sharp and well-defined feature set that was also a characteristic of the handsome bird.

Over time, the child did complete justice to both these titles that he was christened with. He became one of his kind, and true to the name 'Advay', he was unequaled in every avenue that he pursued in life. He also embodied the wisdom, mindfulness, and integrity that we associate with owls- the magnificent birds of the night.

When Advay turned two years old, there was a beautiful new addition to their family. Advay's eyes sparkled when he first saw his baby sister and he gently touched her cheek with his tiny finger. When they brought her home, he wobbled around to help his mother in any way that he could and loved spending hours by the baby's side. He was just learning to talk and tried his hardest to call out her name. The word 'Jyotika' was too much for him to pronounce and so, he abbreviated it to 'ka'. The whole house came alive with his delightfully sweet talk. Right from that young age, Advay seamlessly stepped into the role of a protective older brother who always looked out for his sister and doted on her.

Due to his father's profession and the values that he was taught, Advay grew up with a deep fondness for jungles, along with the flora and fauna that make them their home. The forests surrounding his house soon became his playground, and he used to spend large amounts of his day climbing trees or wandering with elderly tribal boys in the nearby hills & mountains. His mother used to keep a close watch on him during his escapades should he befall any trouble, but she never coddled him with overprotection, or tried to curb his adventurous and risk-taking side. She instilled the confidence in him, right from a young age, that he could explore the things or pursue those avenues that intrigued him. Advay also developed a close bond with animals since they lived in the close vicinity of a forest. He was starkly different from the others around him who were simply terrified of animals for no apparent reason.

He was once playing with some children when they spotted a snake slithering up from a distance toward them. The others gave shrill screeches and started running helter-skelter, but Advay remained still and gauged the situation. He did not think that the snake intended to harm them, and hence he saw no reason to run away from there. One of the boys there tried to throw a stick at the snake when Advay roared loudly to stop him. He reasoned with the boy that the snake was going along its path without making any move against them, and that attacking the snake unnecessarily was wrong and could potentially provoke it to aggression. The situation was thus tactfully handled; the snake moved away from them and soon disappeared into the dense forest, and the children could resume their game.

Advay frequently saw herds of elephants and ambushes of tigers, and every encounter left him in greater awe of these majestic beasts. He never feared them and understood that treating animals respectfully is the key to living a peaceful life within their territory. This lesson came in handy in many other instances wherein conflicts can be resolved by simply understanding and acknowledging the other side. Advay hence learned invaluable lessons in his childhood that he absorbed and implemented in his later life.

However, the biggest source of learning for him was always his mother. He revered her and she was instrumental in shaping his personality to a very large extent. Sridevi always fought for her rights and stood her ground for the things that felt important to her. Her very presence in Melghat with her husband immediately after their marriage was the result of numerous confrontations that she had had with their family, who had tried to dissuade her from going to such harsh terrains and living in an unfriendly forest environment. But she knew that her place was with her husband, despite the difficulties they may endure there. It was a big switch from the kind of life they were used to, but she smoothly acclimatized to her surroundings and embraced everything that was a part of her new life. Some of the adjustments were very small, such as letting go of the luxuries and comforts of city life. However, there were some graver instances that truly put her bravery and resilience to the test.

Anand had once received intel about a sandalwood smuggling ring. He and his team of 4 officers had acted quickly, and trailed and intercepted the goons' route with their jeep. When their futile attempt at bribing Anand had backfired, the smugglers had opened fire and severely injured Anand. They had access to only the very basic healthcare and poor medical facilities in that remote location of Melghat, and these were inadequate for his condition. Sridevi diligently cared for her husband during his month-long hospital stay and subsequent recovery. Her prayers, willpower, and unwavering faith played a crucial role in his recovery, and she was successful in bringing him back from the brink of death. Experiencing and overcoming such moments in her life had defined and honed her personality, and her young son imbibed her excellent traits.

Advay grew up seeing how well she managed not only their household but also the nearby village areas. She worked tirelessly to improve and enrich the lives of the local, tribal women and give them a respectable stature in society as equal members. She had earned their respect and liking and often became a sounding board for them. She was highly distraught upon hearing the overwhelming number of families where domestic violence was prevalent. Advay often used to see her calling groups of women to counsel them and give them hope that they were not alone in their fight, for she lent them a strong voice to speak up against the violence their husbands inflicted upon them.

When asked by her young son about what she was discussing with the women, she would warmly smile at him and say that she was being a good friend to them by supporting them in their hard times and urged him to do so too in his later life. She was a true leader, advisor, and a helping hand to all those in need. She even went the extra mile to learn their language, so that she could communicate better with them. The takeaway from her actions for Advay was to never bow down to wrong and try to help those in need in whatever ways one can.

Advay had a very good bond with his father too and looked up to him. He aspired to become as honorable and honest of a man as his father was. But his relationship with his mother was, and remains an extremely special one. She was instrumental in not only teaching him good values and raising him to be a highly capable man, but she led by example and opened his eyes to what a true leader and fighter looks like. To date, he seeks his mother's comforting words and clarity of thought in the challenging situations of his life.

On a bright summer evening, as the temperatures soared in the forests, the Varma family faced an unexpected difficulty. Anand's duties had called him away from home, and Sridevi was holding down the fort and looking after their two children. Suddenly, a small local boy came running to their place and said that his mother was feeling very unwell. As much as Sridevi wanted to help, she hesitated. Jyotika was too small to be carried there in that relentless heat, and she could not leave the kids alone either. Her heart went out to the boy, but she was stuck in a fix. Just then, Advay walked up to her and confidently said, "I can take care of Jyotika." She smiled at her son's considerate nature, but was still hesitant. "I promise, Ma!" he emphatically said. "I would be very sad if nobody came to help you," he added in a small voice and it brought tears to Sridevi's eyes.

She lovingly touched his cheek and rushed over with the boy. She offered a quick and useful remedy to his mother that eased her discomfort, and Sridevi then ran back home as fast as she could. She opened the door to a heartwarming sight. Advay sat cradling Jyotika in his lap, feeding her sips of water with a small spoon. He gazed up at his mother and gave a wide smile. "She started crying as soon as you left," he told her. "But I thought she must be thirsty. I also feel like drinking extra water these days but I can just ask you for it. I know she cannot ask. So I tried this and she stopped crying!" His compassion and presence of mind impressed Sridevi and she pulled him into a tight hug. "You really are the best big brother!" she said, and his face beamed with joy.

Advay commenced his educational journey at a primary school within the locality. He enjoyed going to school and quickly adapted to the new routine of having to wake up early and be away from his home and mother for long stretches of time. His teachers and parents soon discovered that Advay was a gifted child. He was highly attentive, could retain information easily, and displayed such sincerity that was uncommon for his age. He excelled in every subject that was taught, but he was especially excellent with numbers. His classmates used to struggle to understand the basic concepts, but Advay used to race ahead and wait with anticipation for the new things that he would get to learn.

He had an inherent sense of responsibility and would take complete charge of his own studies, homework, and keeping his notebooks neat and complete. His impeccable leadership skills too must have come forth even then, for he was frequently made the class monitor. He carefully walked the tightrope and managed to keep his teachers happy while also engaging in the carefree fun and frolic that forms a prominent part of one's schooling life. He was thus equally popular among the teachers and his peers and experienced the best of both worlds. Advay was undoubtedly one of the smartest students in class. But despite this academic brilliance, he was far from being a geek. He actively participated in sports & extra-curricular activities of the school such as arts, crafts, and painting. In a short span, he won over everyone with his diverse skills and became the star pupil of the staff and principal of his school.

Chapter 2: The Foray into Rebellion

A few years rolled by and Advay gradually settled and grew comfortable with the numerous roles he was essaying in his life. He was a sensation at school, highly popular, and the role model whom everyone aspired to emulate. The studies too were relatively easy for him since he was naturally gifted, and he became accustomed to consistently being the top scorer. While doing so, he was also outperforming in his non-academic pursuits too, a feat unmatched by any other student. He was pampered at home by his parents, especially his mother, and he was doing things on his own terms. The entire neighborhood adored him, and he was accustomed to receiving affection and attention wherever he went.

It was all smooth sailing, and everything was good. However, as they say, too much of a good thing may turn bad. These were the exact worries that had started plaguing Anand's thoughts as he considered the future that lay ahead for his son.

His own life had followed a rather different trajectory; being a forest official, change was the only constant for him, and he had learned the hard way to never get too comfortable in any situation. He was confident in the power of their upbringing and knew that Advay would never turn out to be an obnoxiously spoilt boy. They fulfilled each of his wants, but in a way that made him realize the value of the things he was getting. But despite this, Anand thought that there were some lessons necessary for Advay to learn to mould him into a better man that neither his school nor his parents could teach him.

He saw a window of opportunity to discuss this with his wife when their kids were not at home and instantly leaped toward it. "I want to discuss something with you," he told her, who immediately came and sat next to him. "Advay is capable of so much more than what he's doing right now. I fear we're making him complacent, and not pushing him to his limits." Sridevi let the words fall over her ears and pondered them carefully. She sat still for a few moments, and eventually slowly nodded. "You're right," she told Anand, who immediately felt relieved that his wife too was on the same page about what he had been feeling. "Maybe we can request the school to allow him to attend some extra classes that can be more challenging for him," Sridevi suggested.

Anand considered this, but the issue was not limited to Advay's education. He had a more foundational change in mind. He shared this with her, and her initial reaction was shock. However, she soon realized that her husband's decision was in the best interests of her son, which is something that every mother seeks out. "I know it's not going to be easy for any of us, but I think down the line he will be thankful for it," Anand consolingly said. Sridevi smiled but her mind was flooded with thoughts; she wondered just how long it would be before Advay developed gratitude for their decision, because she knew that a storm would erupt when they first broke the news to him.

The momentous day arrived a few days later because Anand had taken that time to inquire about the feasibility of what they had thought. After he had been assured, they sat Advay down after dinner one day and told him that they had decided to enroll him into a top-notch boarding school.

Without a second's loss, Advay pursed his lips and yelled, "No, I don't want to go." His reaction had been fully anticipated, and hence his parents remained calm throughout the outburst.

In her own little way, Jyotika too tried to change her parents' mind. "Why does Bhaiyya have to go?" she wailed, and gave lengthy explanations and descriptions to her parents about how good their current school was. They smiled sadly at her sincere attempts, but held their ground that a change would do him good. Advay screamed that it was unfair to him because he was an obedient child and sincere student, and demanded to know why they were doing this. His father tried to explain their viewpoint, but it was falling on deaf ears.

Sridevi too tried to reason with him, but her loving tone and calming words just made things worse. He felt tears stinging in his eyes with the thought of going away from her, and he could not bear the idea. "I won't go," he yelled, and without waiting for a response, he ran out of the house.

Anand tried to go after him, but Sridevi held him back. She had realized what Advay's deepest fear was when she saw him tearing up. "Let me talk to him," she said and went to the place where she was certain she would find her son. There was a sprawling banyan tree near their house that Advay had first laid eyes on many years earlier. It amused him, and he used to hold onto the dangling roots of the tree and chuckle in delight. When he had first climbed it, a delightful smile had graced his face as he absorbed the panoramic view from the top and saw numerous beautiful birds swooshing past him. He had a special fascination for the tree and used to love hanging on it whenever he was not playing with his friends.

Over time, it became his place of solace and thus Sridevi knew he would go there in his time of distress. Sure enough, she spotted him sitting high up in the tree, evidently sulking.

"I don't want to talk to you," he said, with his voice quivering. "Is it okay if only I talk, and you listen?" She took his silence as assent, and asked, "Do you think we would decide anything that was not good for you? Don't you trust us?" she softly asked. He grunted, "I do, but this is not good for me." "You will be living away from me, but you're always going to remain close to my heart. And I promise that I will be there whenever you need me." "No, you won't, because I'll be at boarding school," Advay roared and before she could respond, he swiftly descended and ran off.

The next several days went by like this. Advay stopped talking to his parents, broke things around the house with deliberate carelessness, and vehemently demanded for them to change their minds. But eventually, he realized that he would have to go, irrespective of the number and intensity of the tantrums he threw. However, he was determined to get back at his parents for sending him away, and the spirit of rebellion awakened in him.

Advay soon found himself walking into the magnificent campus of his new school. His father had taken every measure to ensure the credibility of the institute, and it was said to be one of the best. It had great teachers, a very diverse and thorough curriculum, and encouraged students to have a well-rounded education. There was a dedicated hostel wing located just beside an enormous ground. Despite himself, Advay was really impressed with it. It offered almost every facility that he could imagine and the boys staying there seemed genuinely happy. However, he could not understand how this place would open up his eyes to a new way of living, which is what his father had told him before leaving.

Advay had firmly decided against settling in or trying to do well in this school because his mind was still enraged by his parents' decision.

He crossed paths with a senior on his very first day, and that triggered a domino effect of bad decision-making. Advay had disinterestedly sat through an orientation session and his classes of 8th grade were due to start the next day. He was strolling on the school grounds when he heard someone call out to him. He turned around to look at the boy, who wore a gleaming big badge reading 'Prefect' on his chest. The boy held out two of his fingers and summoned Advay to come closer. He was immediately irked, but he went nonetheless.

"You must be new," the boy said. Advay nodded in agreement, waiting for the boy to get to the crux of the matter. "I don't know where you've come from, but your hair is far too long for the polished look our students have," he pompously said and looked at Advay disdainfully. Advay had prided himself on having a thick crop of hair, and his father had already inquired whether it was acceptable for the school. The boy had made a baseless comment since he wanted to flash his newfound authority as a prefect, but he had chosen the wrong target for it.

"Oh, I'm sorry I'm not partially balding like you to have that 'polished look'," Advay shot back, and sarcastically made air quotes to mimic the boy. He was stunned beyond measure and became red with embarrassment. He tried to give a comeback to Advay, but all that came out were angry sputters, and he eventually turned on his heel and left.

"You got him good," a voice laughingly said behind Advay. There were four senior boys standing there, and the one speaking introduced himself as Rishi of 10th grade. "He needed someone to show him his place. Good job," Rishi said while the others nodded in agreement. "I'll do it again if he crosses my way," Advay said with gritted teeth. Rishi grinned at his group and said, "I like you; You've got pluck. Come for lunch with us." It was not an invitation as much as a command, but Advay felt himself getting swept up. Entering the dining area made it clear to him that this was the 'cool group' of the school. Everyone seemed intimidated by them, and he could feel people's eyes on the new boy who had surprisingly been initiated into their clan.

Advay soon realized that his new friends were rulebreakers. They spent more time outside classes rather than inside, and they were notorious for indulging in everything that the school prohibited. When he was first exposed to this side of them, a small doubt nagged at Advay about the kind of people he was interacting with. He thought about his life and friends back home, but those thoughts also gave fuel to the raging fire in him. He decided that since his parents wanted him to learn new experiences at the school, that was exactly what he decided to do. He abandoned all inhibitions and went rogue.

Within a month after he had joined the school, he was initiated into smoking by the gang. His friends had somehow procured a packet and out of defiance, they thought of smoking on the school campus itself. It felt strange in Advay's hands, and he started violently coughing after taking a puff. His friends laughed and patted his back, and though Advay did not enjoy it, he knew that trying it out had cemented his position further in the group. They started indulging in it whenever they got a chance.

Advay was soon also introduced to alcohol, when they climbed over the wall, snuck out of school, and went to a small nearby shanty. On another such instance when they had gone out for a late-night movie, Advay suddenly heard a loud commotion. He saw one of the boys from the group, Gaurav, loudly yelling at a boy. Before he could comprehend what was happening, it escalated into violence. The entire group rushed in to help Gaurav, but Advay hesitated. He had never hit anyone in his life. He recollected the umpteen times he had heard his father say that violence never solved anything. The recollection was cut short, however, for the fight did not seem to be dying down and he had to make a quick decision. He eventually joined in, and for a few seconds while he was engaged in the brawl, he felt like a stranger was operating from within his body and he couldn't remember who he had once been. They trudged back to school and while Advay was visibly shaken over the events of the night, the others were highly callous about it and told him that they frequently got into such fights with boys from surrounding schools. Advay tried to play the part and show how much at ease he was, but his thoughts and feelings were in turmoil.

Among all this, the purpose of why Advay had been sent there lay forgotten. His studies had taken a major hit, as he had lost the focus, drive, and thirst to learn that he once had. The sincerity that had been his crowning glory at his previous school had detached itself from him. If this were the case with any other student, it would naturally entail failing in some, or all subjects. Advay's friends, who found themselves in the same state of distraction as he was, suffered exactly this fate. However, Advay still managed to comfortably pass his exams. He was a naturally gifted student who merely had to read through the pages to comprehend their contents and could assimilate a lot of information in a short span of time. However, there was one aspect of his schooling life that Advay was truly invested in. He was an active participant in every sports competition, debate, quiz, or drama performance that came to his notice.

It had all started off after he saw the immense hype that had been created around one of his classmates who had won some event. Advay had unquestionable faith in his own abilities and realized that he was somewhere craving the popularity and respect that he had once commanded among his peers. Hence, despite being upset about his enrolment in the school and his staunch resolve to not do well there, he worked hard for these extra-curricular events, and over time, he gained recognition as a standout talent.

Advay gradually learned to strike a balance between the time he spent with his wayward group, and the time he dedicated toward academic and non-academic activities. He immensely loved the attention he was getting, but he still felt pangs of loneliness and residual anger that held him back from settling into his new world. On one Friday afternoon, he and his friends had skipped their last class for the week and had sneaked in an alcohol bottle and a few cigarettes. They were at their usual isolated spot near the side gate of their campus. Advay was deeply engrossed in conversation as he took a big swig from the bottle, and held a half-smoked cigarette in his hand.

Suddenly, some movement caught his eye, and his gaze moved toward the gate to look straight at his parents, who were staring at him with an aghast expression.

They had come there to surprise him but instead had received a nasty shock themselves. He had no defense; he knew that he could find no words to justify his actions or regain the trust that he had instantaneously lost. He found it hard to meet his mother's eye, and all the pent-up frustration that he had against his father was suddenly caught in Advay's throat and he could not bring himself to say it. One look at the furtive and guilty expression on his son's face told Anand everything that he needed to know; though it was Advay's actions, it was not his mind behind this and that he had simply fallen in with the wrong crowd.

Anand cast a disdainful eye over Advay's companions, who looked like they did not care much about their misdeeds being discovered. After realizing that their efforts to provide him with a better education and enriching experiences had inadvertently led him to lose everything he had learned, including his values, sincerity, and integrity, they swiftly decided to withdraw him from the school following his 8th grade exam which was imminent.

A few months prior, Advay would have been delighted at this decision, but he now found himself unable to do so because of the way it had happened. However, the deed had been done and Advay's rebellion had extracted a heavy price from him. He decided to never again tread such a path, and work hard to change the unattractive image of himself that had unfortunately been displayed in his parents' eyes.

Chapter 3: The Transformation

In the grand tapestry of existence, every individual's destiny is inscribed with an inherent balance of triumphs & tribulations. One begins to appreciate their place and position in life, and everything they have been blessed with only after going through the lows and getting a taste of where they would be in life if they did not have those things. Advay was in one such transformational phase of his life.

On the face of it, it seemed like he had fair and square won the battle that he had been fighting ever since he had been admitted into the boarding school. He had got his way and was no longer required to study there. However, his victory was far from sweet and had instead felt like a bitter pill that he needed to swallow.

He was overcome with guilt; not due to the fact that his parents had caught him red-handed drinking and smoking on the school campus, but because he had indulged in those activities in the first place. The utter shock and disbelief that he had seen etched on his parents' faces haunted Advay. They had taken him aside and tried to talk to him, but he had nothing that he could say to them. "I never thought my decision would turn out so wrong," his father had sadly said. "All we wanted was to give you a better education and help you realize your potential. I am sorry we wronged you to such an extent that it all came down to this," Sridevi had said with a stony face and Advay felt tears of shame and anger at his actions well up in his eyes.

His poor performance in academics and overall lack of interest in his education had also been exposed after a few discussions with his teachers. With a heavy heart, his parents had decided to withdraw his admission. The traces of their crushed dreams, pain, and disappointment hung heavily in the air, and Advay had felt himself choking up due to the unpleasant situation. The ride back home that day had felt like the most difficult journey Advay would ever undertake. Even in his wildest dreams, he had never imagined that a time would come in his life when he would be too ashamed to speak in front of his parents, and when their eyes would reflect anger and mistrust for him instead of undying affection and pride.

For the next few days, all he could get himself to say to them was "I'm sorry," which they quietly accepted but never reciprocated any conversation. The air in the house became tense. The fun times and lively conversations that the Varma family used to have faded away and gave way to stoic silences. The bond between the siblings, however, remained stronger than ever and Advay's only solace became the time he spent with Jyotika. She did not know exactly what had happened, and she respected her brother enough to not pry about it. Instead, she resorted to offering him her undying love and support and Advay was grateful for it.

Shortly later, his father was transferred to Amravati, the spiritual city of Maharashtra, named after the goddess Ambadevi. Arrangements were made to send Advay to Dnyanmata High School, one of the premier English-medium schools in the city. His past performance in school had raised certain red flags, but his father had tactfully handled it and secured this lifeline for Advay. While informing him of the admission, his father said, "I hope you agree with this decision. If not, please be frank right now itself. I cannot handle another incident like earlier." Advay hung his head and tried to mumble something, but his father had walked away. Eventually came the day when he was to start school, and Advay heard some footsteps while he was getting ready. He saw his mother standing by his bedroom door; he hopefully looked at her, and she finally broke her silence with him.

"The person who went to the boarding school is not my son. I've taught my son well, and he is a much better person than what we saw, and what was described to us. I hope from today onwards, we get our son back." Advay ran and hugged her, and his father too gave him a loving pat on his back that gave him all the strength and courage he needed to embark on this new journey.

Advay joined his new school a little late due to his father's transfer and the delay in relocating to their new house in Amravati. On the first day, he confidently walked into his classroom, but within seconds, he felt uncomfortable. The other students were engrossed in a science class that felt alien to him, and it was clear that their internal groups had already been made and friendships had been forged. He sat alone in the last row, something that he had not been used to, and tried to catch up with what was being taught. Advay was not overtly worried about the studies; despite the setback he had faced, he was confident in his abilities to swiftly absorb new recitations. He decided to give it a few days and tried hard to gel with his new classmates, but nothing changed. They were reluctant to accept him, and he felt increasingly out of place. He eventually went into a cocoon and gave up his attempts to make new friends.

However, fate often has a knack for kicking someone when they're down, and the same happened with Advay. He was sitting in a geography class taught by a teacher named Thomas, who had a reputation for being extremely strict. Advay had been paying attention for most of the part, but he let his mind wander for a mere five minutes thinking about how soon he could leave after school ended.

Unfortunately for him, Thomas sir's eyes caught him daydreaming at that very moment, and Advay heard his name being loudly called out. He was startled, and blurted out, "Y-yes Sir?" "What was I explaining to the class just now?" Advay's brain went blank, and he stood silent for several minutes. Soon enough, he heard quiet sniggers from his classmates and Thomas sir's face became red with anger. "Get out," he yelled, and Advay scrambled out after mumbling an apology.

He felt utterly humiliated; going to school every day was a struggle for him since he had no one to talk to or enjoy with, and this incident was bound to make it even tougher. Now, Advay was fiercely determined to take this in his stride and create a positive outcome from it. He spent every minute of his free time revising the lessons taught in school and even started preparing for future classes. He never wanted to be caught again in a situation where he didn't know his stuff. His efforts brought results a few days later, and coincidentally, this too happened during Thomas Sir's class.

The teacher walked into class and announced a surprise viva test. All the other students started panicking, but Advay remained calm and confident. Thomas sir started with a boy who couldn't get by even the first question. The few students that went after him suffered a similar fate. Eventually came Advay's turn, and he promptly answered the first, rather difficult, question posed to him. He went on to correctly answer almost 10 questions, and he was presented to the class as the poster boy for studiousness and sincerity.

Thomas sir looked at him and admiringly said, "You're a mysterious owl. I have never seen such great improvement in a student in such a short span of time." As his classmates cheered for and congratulated him, he sensed a warmth in them toward him for the first time ever. His face broke out into a wide smile, and that became a turning point for his schooling experience.

Shortly after this, the season for extra-curricular events also started, and it was Advay's time to shine. He no longer felt dull and withdrawn at school and was excited to participate. He quickly earned his way into teams of all sports like basketball, football, cricket, etc., and excelled in each one. Similarly, ascendancy in competitions like painting, quizzes & debates took Advay to a different level of popularity. The most creditable part was that he managed to achieve all this while perpetually being among the top scorers in his batch for every subject. He felt like his life had fallen back into place again; he was doing all the things that he loved while outperforming in his studies and building good relationships with his peers and teachers.

In what seemed like no time at all, about two years had passed, and Advay now found himself at the momentous threshold of his 10th grade board examinations. The air was rife with tension and nervous anticipation, and every student who was preparing for the exams had a perpetual look of worry. The only talk that reverberated around the school was of how well the students would perform, and how their performances would reflect on the institution.

Like this pressure was not enough to instill nervousness, many of Advay's friends complained about how even their homes had no other subject of conversation besides the upcoming examination. Advay could not relate to this beyond a point; no doubt that he too was under pressure to do well, but his parents had been extremely supportive and had tried their best to help him disengage from his studies whenever they spent time together. He had been putting in a lot of hard work but had not resorted to adopting the grueling routine taken on by his friends, wherein they ate, breathed, and slept studies.

Soon enough, he was bracing himself for his first paper and was delighted when he realized that he was very well prepared for every question that it contained. This situation mimicked itself for almost all the subjects, and Advay was beyond satisfied with his performance. As the exams drew to a close, he looked forward to having a lot of time with nothing to do. He caught up on all his activities of interest, like playing sports, artwork, spending quality time with Jyotika, etc., that he had temporarily given up to divert all his attention to studies. He relished and thoroughly enjoyed his carefree days, which led to the arrival of the most awaited or most dreaded day for students.

Advay went with his parents to his school where the results were to be displayed. He nervously edged forward, slipped through the crowd, and reached the bulletin board. His parents were waiting with bated breath; they saw him running toward them and the beaming smile on his face gave them their answer. "Your son is now a rank holder," he joyfully announced, and their pride and happiness had no bounds. Advay had his pick of colleges to choose from due to his exemplary performance. He knew that the college and subjects he decided upon now would have a major bearing on the career paths that would open up for him in the future. Medicine and Engineering were the most lucrative professions at the time, and everywhere Advay looked, he saw people vying for an opportunity to pursue these. He opted for subjects like biology, physics, chemistry, and mathematics that were needed for these streams, and got a place at Shri Shivaji Science College, Amravati, which was the most prestigious junior college in the city.

Advay's first day in the new college mostly comprised of orientation sessions which were intended to get the students acclimated to the ways of the institute, and foster a sense of camaraderie among them. He soon found like-minded people who were easy to get along with and some familiar faces from his previous school. Towards the very end of the day, there was a scheduled interaction session between their teacher and classmates.

Rekha ma'am walked in, with large spectacles and a stern expression on her face. Her keen eyes passed over all the students, and the very first thing she said took Advay by surprise. "All boys from Dnyanmata High School, please stand up." They all did the needful and exchanged curious looks among themselves. "You all have quite the reputation; loud, opinionated, and boisterous." Every single boy from Advay's alma mater, including him, gave a quiet snigger for their teacher's assessment of them was quite accurate. "I want you all to stay in your lane; I should receive no complaints from the girls about you all," she said strictly while peering at them.

She then turned towards the small group of girls in the class. The entire class of 45 students had merely 13 girls, and they had all huddled together in the front rows. "Which of you are from Holy Cross Convent?" 4 of them stood up, and the teacher continued saying, "You too have a reputation. I want you all to mix well with the rest of the crowd; talk to them in a way they will understand and no flashing of high-flown English," she declared.

To Advay's ears, her words sounded like they were coming from far away because his mind had been transported somewhere completely different. He had spotted someone who, for him, was the most extraordinarily beautiful girl he had ever seen. He had never studied in a co-ed school and did not know the first thing about interacting with girls. The girl who had captured his fascination was from Holy Cross Convent; both their prior schools were run by the same establishment, but had a longstanding academic rivalry. He felt like he had already lost his chance due to this.

It soon became clear that Advay was not the only one enamored by the light-skinned and blue-eyed beauty. They silently pined for her without even knowing her name, till one day, someone got confirmed news of her name being Sonia. 'How to talk to Sonia' then became the only thought circling in every boy's mind, but for almost everyone, it remained merely a thought.

The first one who struck gold was a boy named Ashish, with whom Advay had developed a close bond. Ashish was among the most handsome boys in class and had a highly self-assured and likeable personality. He grinned as he joined the other boys, who were wide-eyed with astonishment at his feat. "Piece of cake," Ashish said gleefully. "That seems to be the case only for you," one of the boys glumly replied.

Advay, being a rank holder, earned a lot of respect and admiration from both teachers and students. However, he found it frustrating to experience tongue-tied moments whenever he had the chance to speak to Sonia. He was usually so confident in everything he took on, but his confidence was abandoning him when he most needed it, and leaving him the lurch. Over the next few weeks, Advay kept trying and failing with Sonia, but he was succeeding in the other aspects of building solid friendships, and proving himself as a capable student. They had a series of tests conducted, and the results not only put Advay at the top of his class but also changed his equation with Sonia.

The very last results to be declared were of physics, which had been a particularly challenging exam for every student. Advay scored 98% and was miles ahead of anyone else. He was overjoyed, and yet that feeling was nothing compared to the happiness that coursed through his body when he saw Sonia approaching him.

She smiled warmly and said, "Well done!" Advay was so excited to speak with her that he found himself unable to say anything. After a few seconds of awkward silence, he meekly replied, "Thank you," and hurriedly looked away from her. "I don't bite," she laughingly said, and Advay suddenly found himself loosening up and relaxing. He smiled back and was finally able to have a normal conversation with her. "Can you please help me with physics? I just cannot understand it, especially the new chapter we have started. Have you made any notes for it?" she asked, and Advay handed over his notebook. "Thank you so much! I might just do better than you in the next exam now," she joked, and Advay found himself heartily laughing.

That marked the beginning of an unlikely, yet solid friendship. Before he even realized it, Advay was through with one year of his junior college. Between his friends, studies, extra-curriculars, and spending quality time with his sister and parents, Advay never knew how the days flew by. As he entered the 12th grade, he too felt the level of studies take a sharp hike. He could not afford to slip, for his future course of studies was largely dependent on his performance that year. And yet, as hard as he tried to avoid it, Advay's thoughts had strayed. Sonia had become an integral part of his life; he was used to being with her, talking and laughing with her. Without even realizing it, Advay's feelings toward her had converted into something deeper than a friendship.

34

He found himself actively thinking about her when they were not together, and it made him restless. He found pangs of jealousy hitting him whenever she spent time with other boys, but he never expressed his feelings to her for fear that she would not reciprocate them, and their bond of friendship too would be ruined over it. They often studied together, and seldom must have any student enjoyed studying as much as Advay did during those times. He never knew how time flew by, and she became like an intoxicant for him that he could not shake out of his system. As the exams drew closer, Sonia realized that neither of them was able to fully focus when they studied together, since they frequently got distracted to engage in fun conversations. She chose to prioritize her education at that point, and firmly told Advay that they should resume spending time together once the looming pressure of the exams was over.

On the face of it, he pretended to wholeheartedly agree with her, but his mind was in total turmoil. He could not fathom how she could tear herself away from him so easily when he found the very thought of it unimaginable.

His focus dwindled, and he found himself relentlessly missing her presence every time he tried to study. He was helplessly lost in her thoughts, and filled with the agonizing realization that he was the only one enduring this. The fact that his affection may be one-sided did nothing to prevent it from consuming him in entirety. In fact, he felt more compelled to think and pray about it so fervently that it may materialize. The culmination of this resulted in Advay not living up to his full potential for academic excellence. His 12th-grade marks were sufficient to get him admission to both medicine and engineering, however, he did not remain a rank holder. This terribly upset Anand, but Sridevi was happy that Advay had scored extremely well in the subjects that mattered for admission to Government Medical & Engineering Colleges.

The days following the announcement of results were full of intense discussions at Advay's house. He was eligible for both the highly sought career streams, and there was a difference of opinion between him and his father regarding which one he should pursue. Anand believed that Advay would excel as a doctor since he had been ingrained with values of empathy and compassion right from his childhood, coupled with his acumen for learning. Advay however was leaning more towards engineering. He loved mathematics and was intrigued by the mechanisms and workings of things he saw around him. He truly believed that he would do well as an engineer, for he thought that was his calling. His parents had the utmost faith in their son's decision-making capabilities, and they knew he was choosing an equally good field for himself.

The decision was hence made, and Advay was admitted into the Government College of Engineering, Amravati. This marked the beginning of a new journey that brought with it new experiences and relations that played a meaningful role in Advay's life for the years to come.

Chapter 4: The Losses & The Wins

The year of transition from adolescence to adulthood marks a significant phase in every individual's life. The roles and responsibilities that one has to shoulder in life as a teenager are typically defined. One has to be a loving, obedient, and respectful child, and seamlessly blend this with being a dedicated and well-rounded student. Personalities often shape up within the boundaries set forth by these expectations. It is during the years of transition that come with age and the exposure to new and unfamiliar environments that a person can truly explore their horizons, get acquainted with themselves, and shape up their life and personality on their own terms. Advay too was on the brink of this period of change.

He was fast approaching the momentous age of 18, where a new world that legally permitted him to drive, vote, and essentially make his own choices lay waiting for him with open arms. The life that he had been living thus far was merely the preface of the glorious and awe-inspiring story written in gold that he would craft for himself in the years to come. Like in most other situations that he faced, Advay ably rose to the occasion and wholeheartedly accepted the changes that time brought with it. He had grown up to be a highly capable and handsome man.

Virtues like honesty, integrity, empathy, determination, and courage had been deeply ingrained in him through his parents, and continued to embody these traits throughout his life. His sharp and chiseled features had become more enhanced over time. He had a tall and strapping physique which he maintained well with regular physical activity. However, the thing that made Aday truly one in a

37

million was that he always strove hard to find and unleash a better version of himself, till he felt he had reached his absolute best. The aim was to transform himself into a person he could feel proud of everytime he gazed into a mirror.

Advay had tried his best to keep the claws of disappointment from taking a firm hold on him following the results of his 12th grade examinations. He knew that there was but one person to blame. The surface of his vast academic excellence had barely been scratched, and it pained him immensely that he had not been able to replicate the resounding success he had achieved in his previous board examinations. The glow of pride that had shone out from his parents' eyes, the adulation that he received from his peers, and the relentless praises that his teachers had showered on him in the aftermath of the 10th grade results had been a powerful motivation and he had wanted to live through that phase all over again. Besides the wonderful perception of him that had been created in the minds of others, Advay had felt fiercely proud of himself at the time, and he now regretted denying himself and his near and dear ones the chance to experience those emotions for a second time.

In the moments when he felt like allowing himself some leniency, he tried to reason out that his performance got him into a reputed college. However, these thoughts were quickly dissipated. "The ends do not justify the means," he used to angrily mutter to himself, for he could have gotten into this same college or a better college with a cleaner conscience had he gone about his studies with a more focused approach and had scored to the best of his capabilities.

In a classic play of irony, whenever these thoughts used to overwhelm or unduly frustrate Advay, he found comfort in the very person who had triggered the domino effect that led to his underperformance in the exams. Sonia had become closer to him than ever. Like Advay, her educational path too had landed her at a government college, albeit elsewhere, and they both had a few weeks till their respective courses started. When Sonia had first informed him of her decision to move to Nagpur for her medical studies, Advay's heart had sunk as fast as a boulder in still water. Yet, he had put up a beaming smile and congratulated her heartily. "We should thoroughly enjoy the time that we can spend together, here and now," she had said, and they did just that.

They used to go out with their group of friends, but there was always a special and implied understanding between them that the time later would entail them going out for ice cream, or to watch a movie, or simply taking a walk around the park to have heartfelt conversations. As their plans with the group used to be ending, they would quickly make eye contact with one another to meet at a spot near their college, from where their own plans used to commence. Their bond was like a beautiful secret that Advay housed in his heart; he was torn between his feeling of wanting to keep it so and wanting to proclaim to the world that he immensely adored her. The restlessness that he used to earlier feel about the lack of clarity on where she stood had been replaced with a solemn understanding that she evidently enjoyed spending time with him, and that was enough for Advay to go by. He did not want to rock the steady boat and lose what he had going for him in the hopes of laying hands on something better.

It is said that fate rewards those who are patient, and in Advay's case, this eventually turned out to be true. Sonia was set to leave for Nagpur in four days, and she knew her family would expect her to spend more time with them in the days preceding her departure. She had decided to spend a full day with Advay, and then briefly meet him just before she left. Advay had been taken aback, but he had understood her side. He wanted to make the most of that one day and make enough lasting memories that would hopefully fill the gaping void that would undoubtedly be made by her absence.

They had met early in the morning for a short hike, talked over several cups of tea at their favorite tea stall, and relished lunch at a fancy new restaurant. Advay desperately wanted to catch hold of the minutes that kept slipping out of his control, and soon the time came for them to end the day. They were walking up to her house when suddenly, Sonia grabbed his hand with an urgency and pulled him into a small, isolated lane. "I need to tell you something. I don't want to wait anymore," she mumbled and looked at him in a way that she never had before. Advay knew what she was going to say even before he heard the magical words spill from her mouth.

"I like you a lot, Advay. You are more than a friend to me," she whispered, and Advay felt tingles of excitement course through his body. His face broke out into a wide smile, and he gently touched her hand. "I feel the same way about you. I have for a while, actually, but I was too scared to tell you." "I guess that settles a bet we had once made about who was braver," Sonia joked and entwined her fingers with his. "I want our relationship to turn into something deeper and more real, but..." she started, and then sadly looked away.

"But, what?" Advay hurriedly asked. "I don't think this is the right time for us. We are both young, and we're soon entering a world that is completely new to us." Deep in his heart, Advay knew that she was right. He thought over the implications of what she had said and slowly nodded. "I hate to accept it, but you're right. And I don't want to rush into anything that can create problems for us later," he said, and she nodded in agreement. "Perhaps we should wait it out before officially committing to each other and to a relationship?" Advay agreed and they vowed to maintain their bond even while she was in Nagpur, and revisit their relationship when they were in a more mature space in life. They had decided that neither one would get too emotional on the day that she was to leave. "I want you to very happily bid me farewell because I cannot go knowing that you are sad," Sonia told Advay, and he respected her wishes.

They briefly met on her last day in Amravati, reflected on the fun times they had there, and parted ways with the intention of eventually finding their way back to one another.

Fortunately for Advay, the sorrow of Sonia leaving was soon replaced by the anticipation of starting his new college. He already knew that Ashish too had taken admission there, and he was excited to start this new journey with a close friend by his side. Advay walked through the gates of the Government College of Engineering, Amravati, where he would spend the majority of the next four years of his life. It was a huge campus with many different branches of engineering like civil, mechanical, electrical, electronics, computer, etc. being taught in the same institute. Students from all walks of life came there, united by a common goal to study well and make a good career for themselves. Advay, Ashish, and six other boys whom he knew from his school and junior college formed a group of their own within their branch of civil engineering.

His extended group included roughly 35 other students who had, like him, landed up at the government college after either attending Dnyanmata High School, or Shri Shivaji Science College, Amravati.

Advay remembered the challenging times he had earlier faced due to not having a strong support system of friends in his school and college. Being part of a group wherein everyone stood by each other and had each other's back grew the feelings of enjoyment and contentment that he got in college multifold. He had, once before, been included in a group, but that had paved the way for a downfall for him of a magnitude that he shuddered to even remember.

In a sharp contrast, his new group was a constant source of motivation and encouragement for him. It was either through pure and unmalicious feelings of friendship that they pushed him to do better, or through the light-hearted, and good-spirited competitiveness that they all felt which compelled them to work harder.

The countless stories and experiences that he had heard from others about the unparalleled joys of college days were finally becoming a reality for Advay, both inside and outside of the classroom. The college prided itself on having a highly qualified panel of teachers who were experts in their respective fields. Advay had been introduced to them all during the orientation, and hearing their expertise had filled him with excitement at the idea of learning from these brilliant minds. His classes were several notches above the level that he had been exposed to, but he was hungry for a challenge and welcomed it eagerly. He fared well in the challenge too, as time proved. Right from Day 1, Advay displayed immense focus and unwavering resolve in making the most of this chance that had come to him. He had been lucky to gain admission into a good college for the field of his interest, and he wanted to make it count by becoming one of the best students the institute had ever seen.

In one of his classes, the teacher had decided to digress slightly from the conventional methods. The subject was Engineering Drawing, and the norm of the college was that after every chapter was taught, a small revision test was held to assess the students' understanding. Professor Shetty however thought of testing them practically instead of a theoretical assessment. He posed a real-world scenario to the students and asked them to apply their learned concepts. They were intended to demonstrate technical prowess and ignite imagination. Advay and Ashish were like two peas in a pod; their wavelengths were naturally aligned, and their thoughts and skill sets were well-balanced and complimentary. This made them a powerful duo and they naturally levitated toward one another for the project. They discussed the problem statement, bounced ideas off each other, and bifurcated the work amongst themselves. Advay's mind was racing as he contemplated all the facts, and he immersed himself in the project. He thoroughly enjoyed the process as it allowed him to test the full limits of his intellect and problem-solving capabilities.

Three days later, when they were due to present their solution to the class, Advay and Ashish were confident that they had done an exemplary job.

Every eye in the classroom was staring at them with rapt attention as they took their place at the podium. They had decided to each explain their part of the work, and Ashish went first. The teacher nodded encouragingly at him throughout his presentation and Advay too felt that he had done well. When Advay's turn came, he got completely lost in his explanation and passionately spoke about his thought process, and approach, and proposed an extremely unique fix. The end of his monologue was met with a couple of seconds of pin-drop silence. It was broken by a resoundingly loud clap, and Advay was over the moon to see that the teacher had initiated it. It soon transformed into a thunderous applause from everyone seated there, and Ashish too gave him an encouraging pat on the back. The teacher lauded his logical thinking, ingenuity, and overall flair for the discipline that he had evidently rightly chosen for himself, after which Advay felt like he was in seventh heaven.

Advay and Ashish soon earned the reputation of being the golden boys of their class; they had proved their mettle when it came to studies, and they had charming personalities that placed them at the top rung of the social ladder of the college. They quickly became favorites of the teachers, and students alike.

During the initial days of college, as Advay and his friends concluded an engaging discussion after class, a few of them who lived in the hostel appeared uneasy and kept glancing at their watches. "What's the matter with you all?" Advay inquired. "A group of senior hostel residents have called the first-year students for an introductory session on the hostel terrace at 6.00 pm today. They apparently run the ragging ring there," one of the boys, Shreyas, informed him. "We might as well get it over with," said Irshad. "It is like a rite of passage in college years to face and overcome ragging." Advay suddenly turned to Ashish, and asked with a wink, "Why are we depriving ourselves of going through this rite of passage?"

Given that both Advay and Ashish were day scholars, they were excluded from participating in the ragging session that had been clandestinely planned within the confines of the hostel. However, they decided to experience what a lot of their friends would be going through. They had heard stories of the late night escapades, the bizarre tasks, and the relentless teasing. And so, with the inclusion of Advay and Ashish, a group of 10 of them walked back toward the hostel to live out yet another different and challenging experience.

All the first-year students along with Advay's group were bracing themselves for what was to come and were nervously waiting on the hostel terrace. Soon enough, a group of eight boys walked up to them and said in a booming voice, "Welcome to the real orientation session of your college life." A few of the students shot each other worried glances, but Advay and Ashish looked highly amused at the events that were unfolding. One of the seniors noticed this and directly addressed them. "You both non-hostelers seem to be having a lot of fun. Why don't we start with you?" he slyly asked, fully expecting them to get flustered. Instead, they confidently took a step ahead, Advay asked, trying to sound nonchalant, "What's the game tonight, Sir?" All the seniors were visibly taken aback at their attitude.

Girish, the unofficial leader of the ragging ring with a mischievous glint in his eyes said, "Boy we are going to play many games today. Let's start with 'The Petrified Truth." Advay had heard tales of this game- the truth or dare that pushed boundaries. He looked at his friends, who looked like deer caught in headlights. "Truth or Dare?" Girish asked, leaning in. "Truth", Advay replied with a steady voice. Girish grinned, "Tell us, what's your deepest fear? Advay hesitated; he could lie, but honesty felt like the only way forward, "I fear failing my family's expectations," he confessed. "They've sacrificed so much for my education." The atmosphere fell silent. The seniors exchanged glances, and Girish nodded. "Good answer Advay, I like that." "Now let your friend also join you for the second game" said Rony, a second-year student pointing towards Ashish.

They rounded up Advay and Ashish and set the task- sing and dance to a Bollywood romance song. They thought the two boys would oppose this and take it as a blow to their dignity. However, Advay and Ashish had gone with the mentality to take everything sportingly and in their stride, and not let it impact them personally on any level. Ashish grinned and said, "Alright, get ready for a show like never before," and dramatically started fixing his non-existent long hair to imitate heroines. Advay followed his lead and broke out into song. They indeed put on a spectacular show, owning the challenge put before them.

Their attitude rubbed off on the other students too, who became more relaxed and started loudly cheering and hooting for them. The seniors, whose only intention was to pull their juniors' leg and harmlessly bully them, were left impressed by this dynamic duo. They started clapping loudly, after which Advay and Ashish stopped their performance. They waved to the crowd, and stood upright in front of the seniors; their body language communicated their thoughts of, "We're prepared for anything that you throw our way!" Girish held up his hands and said in jest, "I think I've seen enough. Whenever I hear that song, I'm going to think of you too. And mind you, it's one of my favorite songs, so I'm going to be thinking a lot of you two." Advay and Ashish burst out laughing, and Advay jokingly said, "Glad we could be of service," while taking a bow. Their spirit had pleased the seniors and broken the ice, and they stepped up to shake hands with their impressive juniors. It marked the beginning of a friendship that transcended the boundaries of being senior or junior, which was based purely on mutual respect and camaraderie.

While excelling in his academics and other aspects of this student life, Advay was walking a tightrope and balancing his relationship with Sonia. She was clearly no longer just a friend, but they had not put any name to their bond. After slipping up the first time and letting his studies suffer due to his romantic pursuits, Advay was doubly careful this time around. He ensured that he gave her enough time, and yet never compromised or took shortcuts in his education. They sometimes got the opportunity to talk on the phone, but since she had to rely on her college landline for the same, it was a rare treat. Letters were mostly how they communicated; Advay remembered all the times they had spent together and imagined talking with her every time he wrote to her, for it helped him pour his heart out into his words. He eagerly awaited the post every week, and hearing from her would make his entire day feel special.

The early days were filled with anticipation. Sonia wrote heartfelt letters, inked with her dreams, and sealed with a kiss. Advay, armed with a landline phone and a pocketful of coins, eagerly awaited her calls. The static-filled conversations were their lifelines, bridging the miles between them. Their love was like a fragile thread stretched across the chasm of distance, but they vowed to hold on.

But life had other plans. Sonia's studies consumed her days, and Advay grappled with a busy and complex engineering life. The letters became less frequent, and the phone even rare. Yet, their love clung to the frayed edges of time. But, as time passed by, the distance seemed insurmountable, and the doubts crept into their minds about the future of their relationship. One winter evening, as the sun dipped behind the hills, Advay dialed Sonia's number. The familiar ring echoed through the empty room.

She picked up, her voice a distant melody. "Advay," she said, "I miss you." He closed his eyes, imagining her face—the dimple on her left cheek when she smiled, the way her eyes crinkled at the corners. "Sonia'," he replied, "I miss you too."

The silence that followed was heavy, laden with unspoken words. Advay knew the truth—they were drifting apart. The once vivid colors of their love story now faded to sepia tones. He clenched the phone, willing the connection to hold. "Advay," Sonia's voice trembled, "maybe we should let go." His heart shattered. "No, Sonia. We can make this work. We'll meet during vacations, and write longer letters."

"But Advay," she sighed, "our dreams are pulling us in opposite directions. We're drowning in the vastness of our ambitions." He remembered the night they had decided on a bright future for themselves, their fingers entwined and hearts synced in that dark alley near her house. "We promised forever," he whispered. "Forever doesn't always mean together," she said softly. "Sometimes it means letting go."

And so, on a chilly night, they decided to release their love like a fragile paper boat into the river of time. Tears blurred Advay's vision as he hung up the phone. The ache in his chest was unbearable, but he knew it was the right choice—for both of them. The days that followed were a blur of heartache and longing. Ashish, who knew Advay's story, stood by him in those difficult times. He, along with their intimate group of companions, gradually lifted Advay from the abyss of pain and melancholy, imbuing his days with laughter and his nights with the comforting warmth of companionship. Advay moved on after realizing the fact that the pain of letting go was often the price one paid for growth and self-discovery.

A prominent part of college life entailed participation in student organizations. It was the ultimate seat of power within the college world, and conquering it gave one a special edge and status throughout their time there. Advay knew of 'politics' only as a concept that he sometimes heard his parents discuss, or had read or seen in books and movies. Perhaps if he had been left to his own devices, he never would have stepped foot into that new and unexplored territory. However, circumstances played out in a way that not only did he step foot in it, but gained a strong foothold there too.

Within the student federation, the college comprised two major panels. The first, called the Young Star Panel (YSP), consisted of local students. The second panel, aptly named the Engineers Panel (EP), included students from other districts and cities. This division was intended to instill fairness and transparency in the elections for the student federation. One of Advay's friends, Ravi, exhibited exceptional manipulative skills, coupled with a keen interest in electioneering and a deep understanding of political dynamics. He took it upon himself to engage the entire group in college politics and meticulously crafted a comprehensive framework for the same. He called the first-year day scholar group together at their college canteen, where he outlined his plan.

"We should join the EP and contest the college elections," he announced at the very start of the discourse. His statement was met with a cacophony of raised voices, all of which doubted the credibility of the plan that he had immensely hyped up. If they had to contest the elections, their group would naturally be a part of the

YSP. "I know what you all are thinking, but just hear me out fully," Ravi said, holding up his hands. The noise died down at his request, and they all looked at him with rapt attention.

"Our entire batch, counting all the 5 streams of engineering has around 300 students. Our group itself is of roughly 35, which makes us, right here, 10% of the entire strength. We know that YSP and EP are equal in their numbers, so let's assume that's 50% each. I know this is a lot of numbers, but are you all with me so far?" he said and looked questioningly at his audience. They nodded, and he continued with his grand plan. "I agree that we would ideally be included in the YSP, but just think about this. If our entire group, which is 10% of the batch strength switches to EP instead, the voting percentage of EP would shoot up to 60% and YSP's would come down to 40%."

Advay gradually began to see where Ravi was going with this, and he smiled at the shrewd and brilliant mind of his friend. "We can easily swing 10-15% of the local votes even if we contest elections from the EP. So, looks like a win-win, right?" Ravi said and looked expectantly for praise regarding the brilliance of his plan. It took everyone a minute to catch up and understand the entire proposed plan; when they did, they enthusiastically congratulated Ravi for his clever strategy. "I like to think of myself as a modern-day Chanakya," Ravi jokingly said, while taking a dramatic bow in front of them. Once everyone was on board, the wheels of their plan were set in motion.

The first step was to meet with the leaders of the EP, and secure 5 tickets for the elections for the 'Class Representatives'. Advay represented the civil engineering department, while Ravi himself came down into the political battlefield from the mechanical side.

Other members of their group, Sanjay, Vinod, and Irshad respectively represented the computer, electrical, and electronics departments. The EP leaders too had heard of the positive reputation that Advay, Ravi, and their group at large had among the students. They knew they were a winning bet and readily agreed to give them the tickets. They left no stone unturned while campaigning; they made catchy slogans, designed and printed posters and fliers that they rampantly circulated, and addressed all the right topics that were important for students. Almost every student felt their interests would be represented by this group.

The result was a resounding victory for Advay and all his friends. It was the first occasion in the history of the college that a single contestant had secured such an overbearing majority of votes; given the fact that he had initially been hesitant to enter into student politics, Advay was surprised that he was the one to have secured this historical win. When their whole group met to celebrate the victory, Advay found Ravi and in the spirit of jest, gave him a salute.

"Thank you, my friend. But, I have bigger and better things planned for you," he said while grinning at Advay. "What do you mean? What is better than becoming Class Representative?" Advay incredulously asked. "I'll tell you what is better than that. How about becoming the University Representative?" Ravi shot back.

Advay gawked at him for several seconds; it was unheard of for a first-year student to even contest for the post, let alone win it. "You're playing a prank on me, aren't you?" he eventually said, and Ravi solemnly shook his head in denial. "I was going to talk to you about this a few days later, but since it has come up now, I might as well discuss it with you." They took their place at a table, and soon enough, the entire group joined in the discussion. "You are easily the most famous student of our batch. And known for all the right reasons. You do well in academics, you have a good rapport with all the teachers, and you're in general a go-to and dependable kind of guy," Ravi started, and several others nodded in agreement. "Thank you for the praise, but I don't see what this has to do with contesting for University Representative," Advay said while shrugging his shoulders. "It has everything to do with the elections," Ravi emphatically explained. "You have an actual shot at winning this, and you will be really good at it. And look, you already have a solid backing from the other class representatives, he said and gestured at himself, Sanjay, Vinod, and Irshad. You will need the support of some seniors, and that's where I come in," Ravi said.

Advay was highly skeptical about this; it was one thing to contest for Class Representative, but University Representative was another ballgame. "Okay, okay, don't go around getting too excited about this. I need some time to think. I'll tell you about my decision by tomorrow," he told Ravi to ensure that his over-enthusiastic friend did not take any hasty steps towards the materialization of this plan. He was highly conflicted, and the pros and cons kept outweighing each other every time he pondered over it. As the night came to an end, Advay was no closer to making a choice. His friends had ended up confusing him even more; Ashish told him to unthinkingly take a bet on himself and go for it, but a few others expressed concern that it would be a foolhardy move. As Advay opened the door to his home, his gaze fell on just the person he wished to see.

His mother was pouring herself a glass of water and he approached her. She took one look at his face and asked, "What do you want to talk about?" Advay's eyes widened in disbelief, and he asked, "How did you know? I hadn't even said a word." Sridevi smiled and said,

"You didn't need to. I am your mother; I always will know when something is bothering you."

He proceeded to tell her about the entire discussion with Ravi. "Why are you holding back from participating?" she asked. "Because I'm just in my first year. It is always the senior students only who contest for it." Sridevi heard his response, shook her head, and replied, "I want the real reason, please." Advay quickly realized that it was futile trying to hide the truth from her; she knew him perhaps better than he knew himself. "I am scared of falling flat on my face. I'm really enjoying my social life in college. I don't want to ruin that by earning the tag of the overambitious boy who tried to take on more than he can handle," Advay eventually confessed. "There is always going to be someone who loses an election, right? If everyone let this fear get to them, there would be no competition. For the rest of the college, you will just be like any of these other people to try but fail. You are making bigger implications in your head if god forbid, you lose." Her words resonated with Advay, and he realized that as usual, her straightforward and clear thinking had given him a new perspective.

He thanked her and went to bed with complete clarity on what he needed to do. The next morning, he found Ravi and told him that he was ready to contest the elections. Everything went exactly as Ravi had predicted. Advay's popularity, coupled with the support from the other Class Representatives and seniors swung the results in his favor.

He went on to become the only first-year student to have even won the prestigious title of the University Representative. It felt like he was living out a dream. His friends had transformed the canteen area into a victory celebration for Advay. A huge poster of his photo hung there, and they had convinced the cook to make all of Advay's favorite items on the menu. Advay was touched by the number of people who had shown up to share in his joy.

"Thank you to you all for believing in me. And a very special thanks to my friend, Ravi, who I completely agree is truly a modern-day Chanakya," Advay said to all the gathered audience. His friends then hoisted him onto their backs, and chanted, "New University Representative" while taking a round of the whole campus. Their procession was met with loud cheers from every corner and Advay was in a state of utmost jubilation. He pondered over what his fear of failing had almost led him to give up on, and was grateful that he received his mother's wise advice on time. It was a surreal experience, and everywhere that Advay looked, he could see people admiring and praising him. He promised himself to become the best and most hardworking representative to have ever held this post.

Advay's college was well known for its volleyball team. They had a longstanding legacy of conquering every tournament or championship they entered, and becoming a member of the team was a matter of great pride. Ashish, who had been a state-level player, was immediately chosen and appointed as the captain. Advay had an inherent inclination toward all sports, but he had never had much exposure to volleyball. However, he made a play for a spot in the team upon Ashish's insistence, and he was also selected. He got a chance to travel to many districts and cities for matches, and thoroughly enjoyed the experience and team bonding that transpired there. Over time, Ashish proved himself to be not just a brilliant player, but also a capable trainer and strategist. He was appointed as the coach of the women's team of the college, and he enlisted Advay's help for this task. "I don't know anything about coaching," Advay complained, for he thought it would be a waste of his time. "I will do most of the work, I just need you as an assistant coach. You'll get the chance to hang out with 15 girls every week; you should ideally be thanking me," Ashish said while grinning.

Advay was slightly nervous before the first session; his only real female friend had been Sonia, and he had no intention of recreating the history he shared with her. As he and Ashish were waiting on the court, they saw a big group of girls approaching them. Advay's eyes were immediately drawn to a striking beauty among them, and he happened to see Ashish too staring intently at her. She seemed to be the leader of the group, for she approached and addressed them.

"Hi, I'm Seema. We're very excited to learn from you," she said, and her eyes shifted uncertainly between Advay and Ashish since she did not know who the coach was. She had a pleasing voice, and a very genuine and sincere way of talking. Her gorgeous features radiated when she smiled, and her raven hair beautifully framed her face. She had been blessed with good height and had an alluring figure. Ashish eagerly took a step forward and introduced himself. Seema turned her gaze towards Advay, and he hurriedly explained that he was just there to help.

After a quick ice-breaker session with the team, they started their game and Seema immediately came across as a highly capable player. During their break, Advay happened to find himself next to Seema, and he suddenly felt very self-conscious. She smiled at him and initiated a conversation. "I've heard about you, you're pretty popular in college," she said. "All good things, I hope?" Advay replied and she laughingly put his mind at ease. "Which department are you in?" he asked, encouraged by her warm and friendly attitude. "Computer engineering," she promptly replied, and just then, they were interrupted by Ashish's whistle to resume the game. "I'll talk to you later," she said with a smile, and jogged away. Advay hoped for that to come true for the remainder of their session, however, things panned out in a different way.

As Ashish and Advay stood together at the end of the game, Ashish said in a low voice, "I want a chance with Seema, but I saw you too looking at her. I don't want any of this mess between us, so let's clear it out right away. Can I go for it?" Advay was taken aback for a second, but he wholeheartedly agreed with Ashish that their friendship was above all. "You have my blessing," he said with a grin and firmly resolved never to think about her again. He walked away as Ashish approached Seema, and could hear their laughs becoming fainter as the distance between them grew.

With time, Advay came to enjoy the company of the team. He had formed a close bond with all the girls, including Seema. After giving his word to Ashish, Advay never let his mind stray to think about Seema as anything more than a friend, and it stopped feeling like a conscious effort after the first few days. Advay, Ashish, and the entire team planned frequent outings after their practice, and he had a great time with them. It was his first experience of sharing a pure and platonic friendship with girls, and he had great conversations with them on a variety of subjects. His own game had drastically improved as a result of helping Ashish coach, and he was performing better in every match. The first year of his new college life itself had been a roller coaster journey; he had had wins and losses, learned hard lessons but emerged stronger from them, made lasting new relationships with people, and strengthened old bonds.

Most importantly, he had set himself on the right path to create a bright and blazing life for himself in the years to come.

Chapter 5: Balancing Academics, Family & Camaraderie

The first-year exams marked a significant milestone for every student in the Government College of Engineering, Amravati in their academic pursuits. Coming from diverse educational institutions, where some were overachievers while some were underdogs, they found themselves competing on a level playing field with their counterparts. Their performance in these exams dictated the trajectory of their college life going ahead. Advay and his friends, in addition to their academic pursuits, were actively involved in the student federation's responsibilities, sports, and cultural events. Nonetheless, the college seniors advised them that despite their participation in various activities, they should remain focused and study diligently to achieve good grades and retain the favor of their professors.

The seniors' advice had a profound impact on many of his friends, who were primarily motivated to excel academically by the fear of falling out of favor with their professors. Advay, on the other hand, was driven by deeper and more significant aspirations.

He had forgiven himself over time for ruining his chances of excelling in his 12th grade examinations. But along with the forgiveness, he had made a firm resolve to consistently maintain good performance throughout his engineering studies. He wanted to look back at these four years and have no doubts in his mind that he delivered his 100% in every exam and secured the best marks that he could. In the spirit of this resolve, Advay buried himself under his books in the weeks preceding their final examinations. He covered every topic in depth, and scoured through large stacks of question papers of the previous years to ensure that nothing caught him off-guard. His tireless diligence ultimately paid off; he was the only one from his batch to secure a rank of distinction in two of the subjects and was among the top five scorers in all the other subjects. He was elated. He planned a special dinner with his parents to break the news to them and thanked his stars that he had proved himself worthy enough to see the look of immense pride on their faces.

He had a few weeks to rest and recuperate before the start of a new year in college. It was a stroke of sheer luck that his father too could take a few days of leave during this same period, and they decided to take a vacation to Melghat. Advay had been feeling a very special calling to it; it was, after all, the place where he had taken his first breath and walked his very first steps. His parents were delighted to hear his suggestion to go there, and they all looked forward to spending quality time and bonding together as a family.

It had been many years since they had last been there. Some things felt distinctly alien whereas some others were like a loving and caressing memory that took them all back to their days of living and thriving in the forest. The residential quarters that they had occupied had been converted into a 'Forest Rest House'. It luckily was unoccupied upon their return, and Anand managed to leverage his influence to secure permission for them to stay there. As Advay wandered through the familiar corners of the place he once called home, now completely transformed, a wave of nostalgia washed over him.

He could visualize his mother chasing after him during his toddler days while trying to get him to eat, or caressing his head gently and swinging sweet lullabies when making him sleep. As he wandered out, he saw the spots that were his favorites at one time while playing with his friends. A few of them still lived there, and Advay had a wonderful time reconnecting with them and sharing stories of what they all had been up to over the years. Advay's journey to the remote Melghat jungle was a pilgrimage to tranquillity. Amidst towering trees and silent trails, he embraced solitude, finding joy in nature's unspoken wisdom. The jungle's serene embrace stripped away life's superfluous noise, allowing him to reconnect with the earth's rhythms and his inner self in profound harmony.

On the very first night, while his parents and sister were soundly asleep, Advay was tossing and turning in his room. He eventually abandoned his futile attempts at sleeping and went instead to sit by the window. He gazed out at the penetrating darkness and still silence, both of which were only occasionally interrupted by the glowing twinkle of a firefly, or the sounds of birds and animals moving through the night. As he was soaking in this experience, it was suddenly interrupted by an anguished cry. He was startled and started looking around for the source. The noise persisted and kept getting more and more desperate before he realized it was coming from deep inside the forest. He dashed out of his house in the direction of the sound.

He suddenly stopped in his tracks when he saw that a young fawn had been caught knee-deep in a large puddle of mud. It was frantically struggling to get out, which only caused it to sink in deeper. The frantic and desperate cries were coming from the fawn and its mother who had to helplessly stand there.

With a quick assessment, Advay realized the fawn was trapped too deeply in the mud to be freed by hand. Frantically searching, he found fallen tree branches nearby. Acting swiftly, he grabbed one and fervently attempted to rescue the young fawn from its muddy predicament, determined to aid the distressed creature. In the meanwhile, the commotion had attracted other locals. They saw what Advay was trying to do and quickly joined him.

Five people, including Advay, were hard at work to free the fawn. As they were getting closer, Advay shouted out words of encouragement to keep them going, and they were soon able to save the innocent creature. The fawn quickly moved, ran to its mother, and the two disappeared deeper into the forest. Advay had never felt such joy and his face had unknowingly broken out into a wide smile. He was relishing the moment when he suddenly heard the word 'owl' being repeatedly called out in the local dialect. He saw that a middle-aged woman from the group that had arrived to assist, gesturing towards him and repeatedly uttering the word.

The woman approached him and remarked, "I know you. Your powerful voice and that mischievous yet genuine smile remain unchanged over the years. You're still the Owl."

Advay was about to voice out his confusion when he saw his parents approaching them. They seemed to know the woman well, for they immediately approached her. Advay was told that she was the birth attendant, commonly known as a 'Dai,' who had aided in his delivery. She narrated the origin and significance of the nickname given to him, and then conveyed to his parents, "It's the most fitting name. He truly demonstrates wisdom akin to an Owl, thinking swiftly on his feet. And handsome too, with such sharp features." Advay felt his cheeks redden with happy embarrassment at her praises.

The remainder of their vacation was blissfully spent in the lap of nature and amidst the people who had once been their family. They all were rejuvenated and ready to return to the routine of their city life.

Within a few weeks, Advay's college resumed. He had thoroughly enjoyed spending time with his family and getting to know himself better too, but once he met his friends, he realized how much he had missed them. They had met up a few times right after the end of their exams, however, everyone had their own vacation plans after that which made it difficult to meet up. The whole group agreed to meet at the college well before their scheduled classes began, understanding they had plenty to discuss and reconnect. They each shared their experiences, recollected the things they had done during the vacation, and discussed the new subjects and teachers they would have in their second year.

Professor Archana Thakre, a Civil Engineering faculty member, had gained notoriety in the college for her reputation as being exceptionally stringent and hard to please. The best of students had emerged unsuccessful in their attempts to win her over. As a veteran faculty member, she was renowned in the college for her legendary tales of reprimanding students severely for underperforming in her subject. Advay and his friends already had a formidable image of Professor Thakre conjured in their minds.

The very first lecture that kickstarted their new academic year was scheduled to be hers. They hurriedly concluded their catchup session with their remaining friends and dashed toward the classroom, determined not to be even a minute late. However, luck was simply not on their side that morning. In the commotion and rush to get there on time, one of their group members, Sandeep,

VERSES KINDLER PUBLICATION

took a bad fall on the staircase. His ankle had given way and twisted, resulting in him tumbling down and he was in great pain. Advay and Ashish rushed to his side and tried to ease the pain. "The pain will settle in some time; I just need to sit here for a bit. You two should go ahead though," Sandeep urged them, for he knew that it would create a bad impression if they arrived late. "Not a chance," came Advay's immediate reply and Ashish vehemently nodded in agreement. They exchanged a subtle look among themselves in nervous anticipation of their impending doom.

They knew that they would probably be blacklisted on Day 1 itself in the eyes of the teacher whom they most ardently wanted to impress. Yet, their sense of morality and unwavering commitment compelled them to stay with their friend and prioritize his well-being, regardless of any potential consequences. They ran to get ice from the canteen to reduce the inflammation, and after some time, Sandeep could get up on his feet. They helped him hobble up to the classroom and braced themselves for what would come their way.

As they approached the door and Advay raised a hand to knock, they heard a sharp voice say, "Nice of you to join us." Professor Thakre lived up to every fearsome tale they had heard. She had salt and pepper hair, spectacles that rested on her nose, and a highly stern expression. Advay was the chosen volunteer to explain the reason for them being late since he had an excellent rapport with almost all the faculty members. He felt tongue-tied in her presence, however, and gulped several times before finding his words. "Sorry Ma'am, our friend slipped on the staircase and that's why we could not get here in time." Her eyes narrowed as she heard him out, which gave them all the distinct impression that she did not believe them. "What a convenient excuse," she said. They hovered uncertainly in the doorway since they did not want to assume that they had been granted the permission to enter. "Do I need to print out a special invitation for you three?" she snapped and asked after a few seconds, and they rushed in before she had a chance to change her mind.

Professor Thakre taught engineering mathematics, and the subject too had as notorious a reputation as the teacher. It was reputed to be one of the toughest subjects in the curriculum, infamous for its relatively low pass rates. The class began with an introduction to the subject and an overview of what they would learn. Most students' faces reflected tension and worry hearing about the intricacies of the course, but Advay, who had mastered the fundamentals, felt very excited since he had always loved complex topics. They started exploring the first concept and it was clear that this subject would force every student out of their comfort zone.

Professor Thakre then posed a question that was intended to be a brainteaser. She gave the class 15 mins to ponder over it and try to come up with an answer. Advay lost himself in the comforting world of numbers and stared keenly at the board. His mind quickly filtered out the relevant information and he started scribbling in his notebook. There was pin-drop silence in the room; some students were hard at work to solve the question, while others had quickly realized that it was beyond their capacity and hence sat quietly waiting for the solution.

It had merely been 10 mins and Advay was reasonably certain that he had solved the posed question. He hesitated, however, since he did not want to jump the gun and become a laughing stock in case his answer turned out to be wrong. He wrestled with this decision for a few moments, but ultimately decided to have faith in himself and tentatively put up his hand. Thakre Ma'am questioningly raised an eyebrow at him.

"I think I've solved the problem you presented, Ma'am.",” Advay said, mustering all the confidence that he could. She looked at her watch and again glanced at Advay, this time with an expression of utmost incredulity.

"Do you, now?" she asked, peering at him, to which he silently nodded. "Let's hear it. Please present it to the class," she said and indicated to him to use the blackboard.

Advay nervously made his way there, but once he started with his explanation, he found his nervousness vanishing. He calmly explained how he approached the problem and demonstrated his solution. As he finished, he and all the other students had turned their gaze towards Thakre Ma'am, for nobody knew how to react. She continued looking at Advay for a few seconds, and then she gave him a wide smile.

"I am very impressed; this is great work!" she told him.

Advay felt immense relief coursing through his entire body. He felt he had ruined any chances of having a good bond with Thakre Ma'am by coming in late, but he seemed to have redeemed himself in her eyes. From that day onwards, Advay cemented his position in the rare group of students liked by this hard-to-please teacher. He started enjoying her classes more than he had ever imagined he would. The curriculum of every subject was a distinct step up from what they had been exposed to so far. Slacking even slightly would make one fall far behind in the competitive race that had been kickstarted in the college to secure great marks and remain in the prestigious league of top performers. Advay felt immensely lucky to have an encouraging group of friends around him, for they all pushed each other to do better. They used to wait after college hours to revise the new concepts that were taught, and it was a wholesome combination of fun and productive learning. Due to this, Advay was never overwhelmed with the pressure of studies and could achieve his goal of being consistently good in his performance.

Besides the academic front, he was making great progress in other aspects of his college life too. Since his resounding victory in the elections for University Representative, he had acquired a reputation of being one to look out for in the student politics landscape. Despite being the youngest to have held this position, the way he fulfilled his responsibilities was highly creditable. He displayed immense maturity and complexity of thought while tackling every situation. It took him a few days to get his bearings in this new world that he found himself in. He would initially rely on Ravi's inherent political acumen to gain a deeper understanding of how things worked and would feel the need to have his decisions validated by Ravi. Over time, however, his confidence blossomed, and he transitioned into one of the best University Representatives that his college had ever seen.

Second-year students were also granted the opportunity to run for the post of Sports Secretary. Both the EP and YSP panels were required to nominate their candidates who would compete for the position. From the EP, Advay thought it was a given that Ashish would be selected. He was excellent not just in volleyball, but in almost every sport that he participated in. He was also good in studies and was a highly social and well-liked student. The system was that every member of the EP would put down the name of their preferred candidate on a slip of paper and drop it into a ballot box. The box would be opened after three days, and the student securing the most votes would then contest the elections. Advay went with Ashish on the day of the result announcement with the intention of supporting and cheering for him after the latter's guaranteed win. They saw the chits being taken out and 3 students meticulously working to count all the votes.

"We have the results," one of them shortly announced. "Advay will represent the EP for the elections of Sports Secretary."

Advay was extremely shocked; he had not in the least expected this outcome. He remained glued to his seat for a few seconds while the hall erupted into loud applause. Ashish, who was sitting next to him, grabbed his shoulder and made him stand to go and address the students. Advay walked forward in a daze; he hastily brought a smile to his face and thanked everyone for putting their faith in him.

As soon as the crowd started filtering out, he rushed to talk to Ashish. "I really thought it would be you. I was not expecting this at all," he said. "I am glad it was not me," Ashish sheepishly said. "I don't think that politics is my area of interest. I will do whatever I can to help you, though. I am rooting for you."

Advay was relieved beyond measure to hear this; he had been worried that Ashish too was interested in running for the elections and that this would bear an impact on their friendship. With Ashish in his corner, he was excited to take on this challenge and add another feather to his cap. Advay had the inner confidence that he could easily beat any YSP candidate; however, when Gaurav from the Mechanical Engineering department was nominated from YSP,

Advay was happy that he would be fighting a worthy contender, for Gaurav was an absolute all-rounder. He was the captain of the college cricket team and was a rank holder of his department.

However, Advay had a big advantage over Gaurav, which greatly tipped the scales in his favor. That advantage was the female student population. They formed a significant chunk of the voting population and would play a significant role in deciding who emerged as the winner. Due to the nature of the discipline, mechanical engineering had no girls. In contrast, civil engineering had a sizeable number, and all these were sure to vote for Advay. Additionally, due to the close friendship he had developed with the girls' volleyball team, those 15 votes were also secured by him. They went a step ahead and helped create posters, pamphlets, and fun slogans for his candidacy. They openly campaigned for him and got a lot of their friends from other streams to also vote for Advay. This distinct edge that Advay had over his opponent resulted in him winning the election with a record-breaking margin. It was another milestone achieved by him in the glorious path he was treading in his life at college.

Last but not least, he was thriving in his social and extra-curricular life. The college had recently started drama sessions, where theatre artists came to teach the craft to interested students. Advay once saw his friend Devan deliver an exceptional performance of a famous movie scene, and he too became interested in learning. He joined the sessions and became friends with a diverse group of people. Among them was an attractive girl named Roshni, from the electronics department. She had the voice of an angel and was known to everyone as the Nightingale of the college. Advay found a lot of commonalities with her and they formed a strong friendship.

He also introduced her to Ashish, and before long, the trio began organizing frequent outings together. She was easy to get along with and was interested in the similar things as them, so she loved tagging along with them wherever they went and they too enjoyed her company.

On one particular day that their drama session lasted till much later than usual, she asked Advay where he lived. "I have a scooter. Would you like me to drop you?" she inquired. Advay waved a hand and said, "Don't bother! Deven will drop me." Rohini persuaded him, and Advay sat behind her on the scooter as she gave him a ride home. "That's on my way from home," she exclaimed. "I can pick you up every morning!"

Previously, Advay would come with Ashish, but that very night he called Ashish and informed him that Rohini had kindly offered to start picking him up. "Hmmm, I see where this is going," Ashish teasingly said. Advay laughed it off and said, "It's nothing like that. It's closer for her and it was very sweet of her to offer. You won't need to take a detour anymore," he replied. Hence, Advay and Roshni started going together to college daily. Like Ashish, many others took their bond to be something more than friendship. Rumors started floating around of them being a couple, but they joked about these rumors together and nothing changed between them.

One day, Roshni and her friends were seated in the canteen, tucked away at a corner table. One of the girls asked, "So, tell us! We've been hearing so many people say that you and Advay are a couple." The others chimed in and giggled, and eventually Roshni started talking. "We're not!" she emphatically said. Advay and Ashish were also in the canteen, seated nearby in a cubicle. Neither Roshni nor her friends noticed them. Hearing Advay's name, Ashish touched Advay's shoulder and signaled him to remain silent by putting a finger on his lips. Advay heaved a sigh of relief once Roshni refuted the claims.

Just as they both were about to leave, he heard her say, "Well, not yet. Hopefully, that will change soon."

Advay and Ashish stayed back, with his ears glued to the discussion, for Roshni's true feelings had been a complete surprise for Advay. She had never given him an indication of what was in her heart. The fact that she laughed and made fun of the rumors with him had further cemented his belief that she was as amused by them as he was since they were absolutely baseless. Her statements now, however, changed the entire situation and made Advay question their friendship.

"We honestly started off as just friends," Roshni told the other girls. "But I always loved spending time with him more than anyone else. Just talking with him makes me happy. I don't exactly know when it happened, but I started developing feelings for him." Her confession was met with gushing replies from her friends, after which they dreamily asked her when she was going to tell him. Standing there, Advay was nervously tapping his foot, for the answer would change a lot of things.

"I have not decided," Roshni hesitantly said. "I don't exactly know if he feels the same too. And if he doesn't, it will spoil the great friendship that we have." Her friends intervened at that moment, and all of them started giving their own interpretations of what Advay felt.

"It's so obvious that he likes you too!"

"Why else would he spend so much time with you?"

Advay gritted his teeth hearing their statements, for he knew they were pushing Roshni down the wrong path. He had never thought of her in that way. In his mind, their relationship so far had been purely platonic. He risked a sneak peek toward the table and realized that his fears were coming true. Roshni was immersed deep in thought, and a few moments later, her face brightly lit up and she asked her friends, "Do you all really think so?"

They vehemently agreed, and she happily said, "I think I should tell him soon then!"

Advay had heard enough; he hurriedly picked up his bag and ran from his spot, for he needed a place to think. Their campus too had a large and sprawling banyan tree. It reminded him of the one back in his hometown, which always gave him peace and serenity whenever he sat there. He rushed to the tree and sat down in the comforting shade it offered. He felt very uneasy. Roshni's words rang in his ears and his mind was occupied by a flurry of thoughts. He was in a good place in his life. He was doing well academically, thriving in his extra-curriculars, and excelling in his student political roles. He was blessed to have not just one, but several good groups of friends that included his gang of boys, the girls' volleyball team, and of course, Roshni. But now, it felt like all of this hung in the balance and would soon change for the worse.

His only experience so far in the arena of love and romance had been with Sonia. The initial phase of their story had led to Advay underperforming in a very critical exam of his life. Time had healed those wounds and he no longer thought about it, but pangs of regret sometimes hit him when he remembered that he could have done so much better. The latter phase when they both had put in immense efforts to make it work had ended in sorrow. The decision to end their relationship had been mutually taken, and Advay had known it was for the best, yet, it had not been any less painful. He had tried his best to not let it affect him too much, and luckily, his friends too had been of great help. Despite all this, it had come as a blow to his heart that had taken long to heal. He felt that by pursuing anything with Roshni, he would be exposing himself to a similar set of events, and it was something that he could not afford at this stage of his education.

His chain of thoughts was suddenly interrupted by a voice asking, "What's the matter with you?" Startled, Advay looked around to see that Ashish had followed him. He told Ashish what he was musing about, and what his fears were. Looking thoughtful, Ashish said, "That's a tough one. Roshni is a great girl, and ordinarily, I would have told you to give it a fair chance. But I also understand where you're coming from." Advay sadly nodded and said, "I have decided. I'm just going to give it some time, and hopefully, this whole issue will resolve itself." "What do you mean?" Ashish inquired.

"I'm going to avoid Roshni for a few days. I am hoping that she will rethink her decision, and we don't need to ever have that awkward conversation." Ashish looked highly skeptical, and asked, "Do you think that's the best approach?" "Probably not," Advay honestly replied. "But I don't have a better option currently."

Hence started a period of avoidance and non-communication between Advay and Roshni. Luckily for him, their drama sessions too had ended for the term, and the opportunities for them to cross paths were greatly reduced. Advay told Roshni that he and Ashish were studying together every morning, and so, they would come together every day. Roshni looked crestfallen but did not say anything. Advay made excuses to cancel every plan that Roshni suggested. As much as it troubled him to treat her like this, he thought it would be the best thing for both of them.

This went on for a few weeks. And then, suddenly, the confrontation that Advay had been dreading was thrust upon him. He was walking to the canteen with his group when Roshni came from nowhere and stood facing him. He was surprised and nervous, for he did not know what to say to her. Her face reflected mixed feelings of anger, sadness, and betrayal. "What is your problem?" she spat out. "There's no problem," Advay tried to tell her in hushed tones, for he did not want to create a scene in front of his other friends and the other students sitting in the canteen. "There clearly is some problem. I've waited for weeks, but I want to know now! I can clearly see that you are avoiding me," she insisted, and her decibels rose with every word.

Heads swiveled in their direction to gather idle gossip. Advay knew that anything he said to Roshni would irk her even further, and the situation would spiral out of control. Just then, Ashish stepped in between them and tried to reason with Roshni. "Why don't you both go somewhere private to discuss this?" he calmly asked her. She looked around, noticed everyone's prying eyes on them, and nodded her head in agreement. Advay shot Ashish a look of utter gratitude and went away with Roshni.

He took a big gulp and opened up to her about everything. She stayed silent throughout and stared blankly at him. "I'm really sorry that I hurt you, but I did not see another way," he sincerely said. "Why couldn't you just discuss all this with me instead of completely shutting me out? I thought we were friends," she said in a small voice. "Friends discuss things with one another." Advay had no defense and hung his head guiltily. "I know it's too late, but you're absolutely right. We should talk about this," he told her. They had an almost hour-long conversation where they evaluated their feelings, their priorities, and their aspirations in life.

"I'm just not ready to take on anything right now. I want to do well and make my parents proud. And I don't want to commit my time and attention to you, and then not be able to follow through on it. You deserve better than that," Advay said. She smiled and said, "Thank you for finally being honest with me. To tell you the truth, I had not completely thought it through. I just got caught up with emotions. My studies are really important to me too, and your views made me realize that they could get compromised."

They eventually came to an amicable mutual decision to continue to remain good friends, pursuing their individual ambitions without anything holding them back, and revisiting their relationship status after they completed their education. Advay felt relaxed and at ease after weeks.

Once the awkwardness had passed between them, Advay, Roshni, and Ashish started making fun plans and spending time together. Only now, Seema too had been included in their group. Advay and Ashish had introduced the two girls, and they had immediately hit it off. They used to skip out on some of the very boring lectures and would instead be hanging out in the canteen, sharing stories and countless laughs over tea and sandwiches.

Their time spent in the canteen had made them friendly with many seniors, including the College President, Robert, and the General Secretary, Amol, who were aware of their participation in extra-curricular activities. They were both in their final year and had many amusing stories and tips for their juniors. The Cultural Team, which was composed of students from all faculties and semesters, and responsible for organizing all the events held in college also became friendly with them. One fine day, the head of the Cultural Team called Advay aside. He grinned and told him, "I have a task for you. Are you up to it?" Advay immediately responded, "Yes of course I am!" "Great! You are planning the Rose Day celebration in college," he said and laughed as Advay's expression immediately changed.

"I.. I don't know what to do for that," he stuttered, but just then, Seema and Roshni walked up to him. "But we do!" they both enthusiastically said. "We can help you plan it."

They pulled in Ashish too for the job, and the four of them got to work. They had five days to set up everything, and the girls were highly excited about it. They quickly thought of ideas to make the event fun and engaging, and listed down the items needed to execute their plan. Advay and Ashish were tasked with finding sponsors and handling the interactions with them. The group worked tirelessly. They explored shops for the requisite decoration materials, stayed back late in college to make attractive posters and pamphlets, and worked hard to transform their Community Hall into a special and beautiful place. They racked their brains together for what snacks and beverages should be included and had a great time sampling the items sent by different vendors.

This experience was unlike anything Advay had had before in college, and he enjoyed it. When the day came, their event turned out to be a big success. They saw students thoroughly enjoying every activity they had planned, and the Cultural Team was delighted with how they had managed everything. This experience brought the four of them even closer together, and it was one that they would remember for years to come.

In the meanwhile, the wheel of time had spun and brought Jyotika to the momentous occasion of her 12th grade examinations. Following in her brother's footsteps, she had been an exemplary student throughout her schooling and was poised to excel. Languages and biology were her strongest subjects, but she did not have Advay's natural affinity toward numbers. However, she made up for the lack of natural gifts in physics and mathematics with sheer hard work. She relentlessly tackled these subjects till the concepts too were forced to clear themselves to her, and this way, she had secured a top position for herself in almost all subjects year after year.

In the month-long break before the exams, however, Advay feared that she was pushing herself too hard for her own good. He often observed her eyes looking very fatigued and swollen, saw her frequently press her fingertips to her head as if to alleviate signs of a headache, and her personality itself seemed to have changed. She rarely smiled or laughed with them, and even during family meal times, she would hurriedly finish eating and bury herself again in books.

"Jyotika, why don't you and I go out for ice cream?" Advay asked her one evening, when he saw that she had studied without a break for almost seven full hours.

She barely took her eyes off her textbook, gave him a small smile and said, "I wish we could. I am going to take you up on that offer after the exams for sure."

Advay sighed, and went and sat next to her. She was compelled to keep her book away, and he jumped straight to the point. "I know you want to do well in the boards. But I think at this rate, you're going to fall sick! You barely sleep at night, you're not eating properly, and you've stopped everything else in your life except studying. It's not healthy for you," he gently told her.

Tears welled in her eyes, and she suddenly looked away from him. 'You don't understand...' she mumbled.

"Try telling me," he insisted and sat patiently till she composed her thoughts.

"In the first few days of the study break, I just started losing my focus. I have been regular with my studies all year, so I don't have a lot to catch up to. I thought that a few hours of daily studying would be good enough for me. But when I started, my mind just began to wander. I used to think about my friends, what all I would do once the exams were over, and almost everything else except studies. So, I decided to be extra strict with myself. I pushed myself to study more so that my attention would never wander. And I don't sit out with you all, or go out, or meet my friends because I don't want to think about anything else when I'm studying," she confessed.

Advay knew this was a situation that must be delicately handled. She was tired and overworked, and he did not want to say anything wrong to her when she was so fragile. Like always, he took the route of truth and said, "We really are brother and sister. Our thoughts and experiences are exactly alike. Do you know, I went through something very similar during my 12th grade study break?"

Jyotika's eyes opened wide; she never imagined that her brilliant and focussed brother would have felt the same as her. She immediately felt like she was not alone, and the burden of her tension felt lighter.

Advay proceeded to tell her the entire story. She keenly listened, for Advay felt more relatable to her at that point than ever before. She realized that it was only human to feel distracted, and that she need not be so harsh on herself. Advay's mission was accomplished.

But, at that point, Jyotika burst into tears and Advay feared that he had said the wrong thing. He thought he was making progress, but clearly, he seemed to have pushed her in the opposite direction. He sprung into damage control mode and gently asked, "Have I said something wrong? Please forgive me if I have."

She shook her head and through her tears she said, "You've said nothing wrong. All this means a lot to me, especially coming from you because…"

She paused hesitantly and wondered whether to be so candid with her brother. But it seemed like an opportune time to be real with him, and she trusted their bond enough to open her heart out to him. She took a shuddering breath and continued, "Because I have felt immense pressure to do well being your sister. You were something of a legend at school; great in studies and great in sports. I wanted to live up to your legacy and make you, as well as Maa and Baba proud. I never let myself slip up because I imagined you would never do so. Thank you for being so honest with me."

Advay was stunned. He never knew Jyotika felt pressure due to him, and he was eternally thankful that she had opened up to him so he could help her through it.

"You make us all proud just by being yourself," he lovingly said. "You should never take pressure to match anyone, especially not me! You are great at so many things that I cannot even try to do. And remember, while these marks are important, they do not define you. You're an extremely smart, capable, and hardworking girl. You're going to do well in life, whatever be the numbers that may show on your papers," he smiled, and it was just what she needed to hear. She hugged him and he affectionately ruffled her hair.

The entire family spent a fun evening together after weeks. They devoured the delicious meal prepared by Sridevi, watched a movie, and played cards. Anand asked his daughter what had caused this change in her and why she had agreed to take this much-needed break from her studies. She winked at her brother and said, "Someone told me that marks don't define me. It's the best advice I have heard in a while!"

Advay grinned at her, overjoyed to see his sister relaxing, enjoying the small but significant joys of life, and was glad that he could impart some wisdom that helped her.

The wisdom and support received from her brother made the remainder of Jyotika's preparatory leave much more rewarding. Instead of cramming her exhausted mind with more information, and pressuring it to perform well in such dire circumstances, she developed a healthier relationship with her studies. Advay worked with her to create a new timetable, one that would ensure she got the requisite amount of studying done while also prioritizing her health and well-being. Besides the schedule, he also helped her with tips and tricks on how to study smartly.

Her prior approach was more focused on mugging up instead of developing a deeper understanding of concepts. And luckily for Jyotika, Advay was a master of the very subjects that she found the most difficult. He dedicated a lot of time to helping her with physics and mathematics, which were the subjects that scared her the most. The very sight of the complex problems and intimidating numbers would make her break into a cold sweat, but after a few study sessions with Advay, that changed. He strengthened the foundation of her knowledge in those subjects and presented every concept in a way that could easily be memorized. She became more relaxed and at ease with herself, having let go of the mounting pressure that she was burying herself under.

Her first exam was mathematics. In all prior situations, the day before a maths paper was spent in anxiety and nervousness, with her face buried in books till the very end. This time, however, she followed Advay's schedule and firmly kept her books away at 6 o'clock in the evening. She spent time with the family, had a good night's sleep, and woke up refreshed and ready.

Advay, Sridevi, and Anand all waited with bated breath for her to return from the exam. They glanced at the clock repeatedly. and exchanged nervous glances with one another as it ticked away. They were worried that the exam had not gone well, and were scared for how Jyotika would take it. When the door eventually swung open, however, Jyotika walked in with the widest smile on her face and a box of Advay's favorite sweets in her hand.

"It was a success!" she excitedly announced. "The questions made more sense to me, and I could easily do the calculations because of that." She looked toward Advay, held up the box of sweets, and warmly said, "And all credit goes to my wonderful teacher. He helped me in more ways than I can ever express, and I will be forever grateful for it."

Advay's heart swelled with pride and joy. They all celebrated and relished the sweets, and Advay felt a sense of accomplishment like never before.

Chapter 6: Celebrations, Challenges & Confrontations

After playing a significant and positive role in the momentous time of Jyotika's board exams, Advay found himself on the brink of adulthood, nearing his twentieth birthday. It was a joyous occasion and his family and friends were keen to celebrate the day with him.

"What do you feel like doing?" Sridevi asked her son over breakfast one morning. 'Should we plan a short family outing somewhere? Or would you like to invite your friends for a nice celebratory lunch or dinner?" she suggested.

Advay gently shook his head and replied, "Neither! I have something else in mind."

He told his family about his idea for a birthday celebration and they absolutely loved it. He wanted to celebrate his special day in a unique and meaningful way; one that would leave a lasting impact on society. He had thought of organizing a tree plantation drive. The inspiration came from his father and his upbringing; he wanted to give back to nature since he had spent countless hours amongst trees and some of his best childhood memories were housed in the dense jungles of his hometown. Thus, he envisioned planting 2000 saplings of fruit-bearing trees that would bring purity, freshness, and sweetness to the city at large.

Advay knew this would be a daunting task, but he was determined to see it through. He reached out to the Principal of Navodaya Vidyalaya, Amravati, located close to Advay's college. The Principal, who shared his enthusiasm for environmental conservation, loved the idea and immediately agreed to join hands with Advay for this noble cause. Advay also contacted the forest authorities, who provided him with the necessary permissions, guidance, and the required fruit saplings.

He informed Ashish, Seema, Roshni, Ravi, and a few more of his college gang about his plan & they gathered at a barren stretch of land close to the college campus on the morning of Advay's birthday. The Varma family was already along with the school children and staff, proud of Advay's initiative. The sun was already high in the sky. Advay divided the complete gathering into smaller groups, each responsible for planting specific types of fruit trees—mangoes, guavas, papayas, and many more.

As they dug holes and gently placed the saplings, Advay felt a sense of purpose. He imagined those tiny plants growing into mighty trees, providing shade, oxygen, and succulent fruits for generations to come. The sweat on his brow was a badge of honor, and the mud stains on his cheeks were a symbol of his everlasting devotion to Mother Earth.

News of the tree plantation moved fast through the whole city. Local media outlets swarmed in, much like bees drawn to honey, to cover an event, the likes of which had never been seen before. The group continued their work throughout the day, and its enthusiasm only rose as the sun dipped closer to the horizon. By sunset, all 2000 saplings were in the ground. Advay stood amidst the newly planted trees, feeling a mix of exhaustion and exhilaration.

The next morning, the local newspapers carried headlines like, 'A Green Birthday Bash: 2000 Trees Planted!' and 'Young Adult Turns Environmental Hero!' The story touched hearts and inspired many others to take up similar projects. Advay received invitations to speak at environmental conferences and schools. His college too awarded him a special commendation for his outstanding contribution. However, the best and most cherished outcome of his novel birthday celebration remained the pleasing vista that blessed his eyes whenever he passed by the spot of their plantation drive.

After he basked for a few weeks in the enjoyment and success of his novel celebration, the time drew closer for him to sit for his second-year assessments. He had consistently done well the whole year, be it in projects, assignments, or surprise evaluations. He was consumed by a fierce desire to see it through till the end, and perform exceptionally in the final exams too so as to end the academic year on a high. His sharp mind and relentless efforts supported him in this quest and he passed every paper with flying colors.

Before he even realized it, half of Advay's engineering education was complete and he was ready to kickstart his third year. The four-year-long journey that he had embarked upon had, at one point, felt lengthy and tedious. However, he had blended into his new world with the same ease as a blooming plant takes its place within a forest. He had grown and thrived in every aspect of this new phase of his life. His academics, sports, cultural, and political activities were all of a diverse nature and demanded their fair share of time and attention. Striking a balance between all these was like walking on a precarious tightrope. Few would have managed to do it as well as Advay did.

Right from the inception of the new academic year, the wheels were set in motion for a riveting political season that was sure to bring its share of drama, intrigue, and excitement. The key players were geared up. They had their roles defined and their ambitions spelled out; each one knew exactly which position they wanted to be in as the season drew to its magnificent close. Some experienced members and decision-makers of the EP, who were determined to secure a resounding victory for their party, gathered to chalk out their game plan. The preliminary step was to identify a candidate suitable to contest the elections for General Secretary, which was among the most coveted posts in the world of college politics.

"We need to put up someone who can secure a guaranteed win. There are rumors that the YSP candidate is Vishal Shah. He is a very strong candidate, and we need someone stronger," said the Party President, Rajesh Kumar.

What followed his declaration was an intense discussion about the likely candidates. All these were from the final year since it was an unsaid rule of the elections that the honor of contesting for General Secretary was reserved for the senior-most batch. Every candidate they considered had some drawbacks; some excelled in their academics but lacked popularity, while some had a great rapport with other students but lacked the inherent analytical thinking and sharpness needed to excel in politics.

"What about Advay Varma? I think he is perfect; there isn't one single criterion that he does not meet," asked Minal Gupta, who was the defacto strategist for the party. She continued, listing out the reasons for her unusual suggestion. "He secured the most epic win we have ever seen in the history of the college for the University Representative elections; it was a clean sweep. And he did good work too. He's extremely well-liked, has proved that he can make quick and smart decisions, and is an all-rounder. He's been one of the best Sports Secretaries too that we've had."

Many heads slowly nodded in agreement, but Rajesh looked hesitant. "He is a third-year student. This usually never happens," he said.

"We've usually never had such a great candidate either. I think he is someone worth changing the norms for. After all, we want to win. I think he can get us there," Minal countered, and her compelling argument eventually convinced the skeptics. Advay was the chosen EP representative for General Secretary.

When they made their announcement, Ravi, Ashish, and many other members were overjoyed. They hooted loudly, shouted their EP slogan in celebration, and cheerfully thumped Advay's back. Advay however, had a forced smile pasted on his face, for nervousness had taken over his entire being. Once the celebration quietened down, he pulled his closest aids aside to discuss his dilemma with them.

Before Advay could even get out a word, Ravi held up his hand and said, "I know exactly what's on your mind. I guessed it immediately from your expression when Minal and Rajesh came to talk to us. You're worried because you are the first-ever student not from final year to contest these elections."

Advay gulped nervously and nodded, "You're absolutely right."

Ravi sighed and said, "I know it is really unlikely. But I think you have a real shot at this, irrespective of which year you are in. And elections are about choosing the right candidate, which you surely are."

"Besides, the party too must have thought about these implications before making their decision. If they are not worried about it, I don't think you should be," Ashish contributed.

Advay knew their arguments had merit, but deep down, he was still uneasy. As happy as he was about his selection, he could not shake off the feeling that it had triggered a cascade of negativity and chaos that would soon descend upon them.

Unfortunately, his worst fears came true.

As the news of Advay's candidacy spread, it irked many seniors from the EP who felt that irrespective of his merits, a third-year student did not deserve to fight for the post. A group of them, led by an egotistical and arrogant boy named Amar, questioned Minal, Rajesh, and the others who had made the decision. In reality, Amar himself was expecting to get chosen, and he felt insulted that a junior had been chosen over him. He angrily yelled that Advay was a wrong choice, and was blindly supported by his followers. However, the EP decision-makers stuck to their ground. They tried their best to make Amar see that it was all for the benefit of the party and that he should not take things personally. But the damage was done.

On the very next day, as Advay and his friends walked into the college campus, they saw a large crowd gathered near the auditorium. They exchanged quizzical glances at one another and tried to move forward to get a better look. Just then, they saw Amar walk toward the group, holding several chart papers, marker pens, and cello tape in his hand. Advay had been apprised by Minal and Rajesh about the argument they had had with Amar, and hence he was not surprised when Amar shot him a very dirty look. That look instantaneously transformed into a snigger, and he wordlessly blended into the crowd. Through a small gap that had formed as a few people walked away, Advay saw that Amar and his group were hard at work making campaigning material like posters and pamphlets for Vishal, the YSP candidate. They did not just stop there. They loudly started having an internal discussion that was evidently meant to be overheard by the onlookers of their stunt.

"There's a reason only fourth-year students are chosen for General Secretary elections," Amar proclaimed. "Anyone else simply does not have the maturity, and frankly the common sense to get the job done. And I think third-year students are the absolute worst. They think they've done a lot and know a lot, but they are nothing. Meaningless specks on the larger picture."

The words were an unabashed provocation, intended to demean Advay and his candidacy and bring forth some negative reaction from him. A few others from Amar's group joined in, each making baseless comments that only further highlighted how egotistical and cocky about themselves they were.

However, they had chosen the wrong bait, one who would not be caught so easily in the trap they were desperately laying for him.

Ashish and Ravi were closely looking at Advay, gauging how he would react to their taunts and the declaration of war against him. They were prepared to step in if their friend lost control and tried to pick a fight, and hence they were surprised when Advay looked at them with a cheeky grin and held out his hand to convey that he had had control over the situation.

Matching the raised pitch that his opponents used, Advay made his move in this battle of wits and said to his friends, "Maybe third-year students are not the best; which makes me more so pity those who can't win against them. You think you're a big shot in student politics, but your own party can't trust you. They choose a meaningless speck over you for the elections that you've been trying so hard for. It's sad, really."

His words cracked like a whiplash, and their effect was clearly discernible. The students gathered around started loudly sniggering, and many of them patted Advay's back or gave him a playful clap to show their solidarity and support. Ashish and Ravi were stunned at Advay's quick-witted and sharp response and marveled at the way he handled the situation. Amar's face took on a deep shade of red and he stared angrily at the crowd that was mocking him and his failed efforts to shame Advay. In a final, desperate attempt to salvage the situation, he firmly put up the poster for Vishal and raised a balled fist while shouting, "Vote for Vishal!" He hoped that more people would support his cause, but he heard only a handful of his friends meekly echoing his chant. He gathered his things, gave Advay and his group a menacing stare, and stomped off.

As Advay, Ashish, and Ravi went toward their classrooms, they crossed Rajesh and briefly recounted the events of the morning.

Rajesh gave a deep sigh and said, "We knew Amar was unpredictable and petty, but we never thought he would resort to such measures. Campaigning for the opposing party's candidate is the lowest level one can stoop to."

Advay's face was marked by concern as he asked, "Are you sure we should go ahead with my candidacy? I feel we've triggered a domino effect that will affect the entire election season. Do you think it's worth it?"

Without even thinking for a second, Rajesh replied, "You're worth it. And not just me, but a lot of people in the EP and in the college think that."

Advay was grateful for the undying faith that Rajesh, Minal, and the others from the EP had shown in him. He knew his path toward winning the post of General Secretary would be far from simple or straightforward. It would be full of many more obstacles, and Amar's discontent was just one of them. But he was a fighter who could look obstacles in the eye as he forged ahead to his goal, without letting anything stop him. The confidence that so many people had in him fired his resolve to tackle every challenge that came his way. For him, winning or losing did not matter as much as the attitude with which he fought. His parents had instilled this mindset in him and it helped him in almost every difficult situation. He would put his heart and soul into contesting the elections, for that was the only thing in his control. The results would be determined by fate, but he would happily accept any outcome due to the knowledge that he had left no stone unturned.

Advay's foretelling that the dynamics of the election season would be affected came true a few days after he started his campaigning. He spent almost all his free time interacting with students, understanding their concerns, learning about the aspects that mattered to them, and trying to embody the ideal traits they wanted in a General Secretary. One day, as he finished a discussion with a large audience, a group of students from electrical engineering came up to him.

"We're from the YSP, so we didn't attend the discussion. But now, we're hoping we would have. We overheard some parts of it and we really like your ideas. We think you're a great candidate," one of the girls said.

Advay smiled warmly and replied, "Thank you, it really means a lot."

The girl hesitated briefly and continued, "We want to back you in the election. I know it's not common, but we know our candidate is being openly supported by some people from your party. They are doing it because they are fourth-year students. We all are in our third year, so we have the equal right to support you."

Advay was at a loss for words. As happy as he was about the overwhelming appreciation, he knew this would open a new can of worms. He was about to voice out his concerns when Ravi, who was standing next to him, hurriedly said, "Of course you have the equal right to support him! You're making the right choice," he assured them.

As the group cleared away, Advay tugged on Ravi's arm and said, "Why did you encourage them? It's just going to complicate things now. YSP students openly supporting EP candidates and vice versa; it's unheard-of during elections."

"I know, but they approached us in good faith. If they truly feel you're the better candidate, they should be able to support you," Ravi countered, and Advay had nothing to refute that reasoning.

Advay's dedicated effort toward campaigning produced results in due time as more and more people became influenced by his clear vision and courage, and expressed their support to him. However, complacency was something he could not afford. He kept thinking of ways in which he could do better and get more people on his side. During one of their brainstorming sessions, Ravi looked lost in deep thought. Advay poked his arm with a pen to shake him out of his daydreams, and asked, "What are you thinking about?"

He looked startled at this interruption in his flow of thoughts and said, "I'm thinking about Keshav and his gang." They were a large group of twenty-three people from the third year who supported the YSP. In response to Advay's questioning glance, Ravi continued, "They form a significant portion of YSP's supporters. If we can get them over to our side, your win is guaranteed."

Advay pondered what Ravi said and slowly nodded. "I agree, but getting them over to our side won't be easy. They are high on party loyalty; I don't think they will switch over for any reason."

"I think I can give them a strong enough reason, something that makes even the most determined people change their minds," Ravi said with a devilish smile. He explained himself without words as his hand held an imaginary class that he dramatically sipped from and swayed his head in delight.

Advay looked aghast at the suggestion. He knew that such forms of in-kind bribery were common during college elections. However, he feared that by resorting to them at this stage, they would risk losing everything that they had worked hard for so far. He voiced his concern and said, "I can't be involved in things like this, it will give a very bad impression. And we've worked too hard to risk something like this now."

Ravi solemnly nodded and replied, "Correct, you cannot be involved and you won't be. But we can."

He looked over at Ashish, who was keenly listening to the whole discussion. They exchanged a smile, and Ashish said to Advay, "Forget you ever heard this conversation. You're not a part of it in any way." Advay tried to protest the idea, for he did not want them to get in any trouble while he was shielded due to his lack of involvement. It was to no avail as their plan was quickly decided and they refused to abandon it since they knew it would secure a win for Advay.

Their plan was timed for the night prior to the voting when they invited Keshav and the others to a small restaurant on the outskirts of Amravati city under the pretense of an organized get-together to unwind from the hectic election campaigning. The temptation of free alcohol drew the entire gang there. After exchanging a few pleasantries and ordering a large number of drinks, Ashish, Ravi, and a few others who were in on the plan got to work. In the middle of conversations, they subtly brought up Advay's candidacy and how his victory would benefit all students, without giving away that the sole reason of the party was to swing their votes in his favor.

As the drinks kept flowing in, the discussions became more insistent and persuasive; Ashish and Ravi shed their cloak of disguise and openly became advocates for Advay's candidacy. However, their audience was, like Advay had predicted, fiercely loyal to their own party. While they acknowledged that Advay was a worthy candidate and deserved to win, they remained hesitant to contribute to his victory. Engrossed in the debate that ensued, with both sides passionately putting forth their points, they lost track when their alcohol consumption went up from a few glasses to several bottles.

"We're all too heavily drunk right now. I don't think it's a good idea for us to drive back in this state," Ravi said.

Keshav, with his eyelids weighed down with sleep, asked, "I agree, but what else can we do?"

"Don't worry, I know the owner of this restaurant. He will make some arrangements for daris and some of us can adjust on sofas," replied Ravi. Everyone agreed and decided to stay back for the night at the restaurant.

Ashish woke up with a start the next morning and realized that it was already seven o'clock. The voting was to start at 8:30 AM and the college was an hour away from the restaurant. He looked around and saw that everyone else was asleep, and they reeked of alcohol. He hurriedly splashed water on his face and freshened up, and then proceeded to wake up Ravi and their other friends. As they came to their senses, they tried waking up a few of the boys, but nobody stirred. The clock was ticking and they needed to act soon.

Ashish emphatically said, "We need to keep them here, at least till the voting is over. It's not our fault that they drank beyond a point that they can handle. If they miss the elections, it's not on us."

Ravi solemnly nodded, for he saw the practicality of what Ashish suggested. With this, they both took a mutual decision that everyone else agreed with. They silently moved through the room, stepped out, and bolted the door behind them.

In the meanwhile, a group of senior YSP members, joined in a malicious alliance with Amar and his gang, closely kept track of the voting. They had taken every measure, some fair and some unfair, to keep Advay away from the embrace of victory. They had been thwarted at almost every step by Advay's growing popularity, but they had relentlessly tried.

As Ashish and the others walked in, one of Amar's friends urgently revealed, "I saw this Ashish and Ravi hanging out with Keshav very late last night. I was driving by, and I saw them from the window of the restaurant. It was a big group, and they were drinking a lot."

They immediately realized that it was an attempt to get Keshav and his group to vote for Advay. One of the YSP members though waved a dismissive hand and said, "I'm not worried about Keshav. He is a straight shooter; there's no way he will betray his party."

"That's all well and good, but where is Keshav?" another YSP member grumbled. They waited for a long time and eventually, two of them were sent to locate Keshav and his group.

However, they were too late as the voting drew to a close and counting commenced. The remaining members of the malicious alliance waited eagerly for some news about Keshav and his group's whereabouts, but it was soon announced that the results were ready. They could do nothing to stop the process and they waited on the sidelines with growing rage.

The student in charge of announcing the results took her place at the podium and said, "First up, your new President is Omkar Bodke from the YSP." The announcement was met with loud cheers and excited cries, for the most deserving candidate had won the post. Soon after, results for the elections for Sports Secretary, Joint Secretary, and Magazine Secretary were announced.

"And now, coming to the General Secretary," she said, and her words were met with a sudden and still silence. "This election season had a lot of different things. We deviated from a longstanding tradition of keeping this post reserved for seniors, and I think it was for the good. You all seem to agree too, for the clear winner and your next General Secretary is Advay Varma from the EP!"

Hearing his name being called out was a feeling beyond surreal for Advay. Given how difficult this particular season was, the jubilation felt sweeter and more special. He looked around at the people without whom he could never have dared to dream of a victory. He hugged Ashish and Ravi and joined in the loud and happy cheers coming from his other supporters. While he was celebrating the win, it still felt unreal. He wondered if he was in a dream that would be broken any minute to take away the victory from him. But as he looked at the joyous faces surrounding him, and heard the delighted cries of his name that echoed all around, he knew this victory was etched in stone and could not be snatched away from him.

His political rivals seethed in anger. They had uncovered the truth of the previous night's events, though they had a misplaced understanding of it. They were convinced that Ashish, Ravi, and the others had always planned to lock up Keshav and his group in the restaurant so as to prevent them from voting. They felt cheated and believed that the voting process was rigged. They vowed to take their revenge and disrupt the celebrations that they felt Advay did not deserve.

A party was planned for Advay's win at their college canteen. It was decorated with festive balloons and streamers, courtesy of Seema, who took it upon herself to transform their canteen into a grand party hall. It was intended to be a surprise for Advay who assumed that the celebrations had ended along with their day in college. His friends planned the whole event, and the idea was to call Advay to college under a false pretense. Ashish, Ravi, Irshad, Vinod, Sandeep, and their entire gang, along with Seema, Roshni, and a few other girls from the volleyball team had gathered there. The air was buzzing with excitement and everything was ready for Advay's arrival.

However, parallel to their plan, another evil one was set in motion. Amar had overheard a few people discussing about the party and he thought it was the perfect time for Advay and his companions to be taught a harsh lesson. The malicious alliance got together once again to lay a trap.

The group excitedly waiting at the canteen was startled by the sound and sight of many bikes aggressively coming toward them. Before they had any time to react, a group of goons was upon them. The girls shrieked in shock and ran behind trees for cover. The goons beat up Ashish, Ravi, and the others, who fiercely retaliated and a fight ensued. The party that was intended to be filled with sounds of laughter and joy instead had sounds of kicks, punches, and loud and vicious cries. When the goons sensed that their opponents had no intention of backing down, despite being badly hurt, they quickly decided to leave before the fight attracted any onlookers.

As they sat on their bikes and raced away, Advay walked past them. He wondered who these hooligans were and why they were on the campus when suddenly he noticed the sight before him and his heart went cold.

His friends were covered in blood, and had deep cuts and bruises all over. Their canteen, which was clearly decorated for what he realized was a surprise party for him, had been vandalized and left with broken tables and chairs.

He raced over to Ashish, and asked, "Are you alright? Who did this?"

Ashish managed a feeble smile and replied in a low voice, "I am okay. You should see the other guys."

But through the forced joke, Advay saw a deep gash on his cheeks and lip and saw that he could barely sit up. It was the same for the others, though they all tried to downplay the severity of their injuries. Advay felt fury rise in him; he did not know for sure but he had a sneaky suspicion of who could be behind this underhanded attack on his friends during a party hosted for his victory celebration. Suddenly, from afar, he caught sight of Seema peeking out from behind a tree. Fear took a renewed hold of him as he ran toward her, worried out of his wits for her safety.

"Did they come close to you?" he asked, once he saw that she had no visible injuries on her. "Please tell me you're okay," he urgently said, since she was too shocked to respond. She then nodded and finally found her voice to say, "I'm okay. We all hid behind the trees."

Advay then noticed the other girls, and he gently escorted them all away from their place of refuge. He left his injured friends in their care and quickly went to the hospital wing of their college to gather supplies for first aid. He tended to Ashish's and Ravi's wounds, which were the most severe, while the girls took care of the others.

He then asked for his father's help to get them all home safely, and the Varmas reached there within minutes. Sridevi and Jyotika offered to drop the girls home, while Advay and Anand dropped all the boys.

After ensuring that each of them was safe and sound in their houses, Advay prepared a small care package for them, with fruits, chocolates, and some medicines, and went all across the town to give them. He discussed his suspicions with Ashish at his home, who immediately agreed that only the malicious alliance could be behind such a stunt.

"What are you planning to do?" Ashish asked, for he saw rage burning in his friend's eyes and noticed Advay's jaw was tightly clenched.

"I am planning a payback," Advay replied, and in his mind, he had a plan drawn out to achieve it.

The next day, he went to visit an old friend, one whom he thought he would never cross paths with again. Ratan Singh, who was a part of Advay's group in boarding school, had become a local kingpin. He explained the entire situation and asked for some weapons and manpower to help him avenge his friends. Knowing that Advay was doing it for the correct reasons, and not initiating an unprovoked attack, Ratan immediately agreed to provide the help he asked for.

Armed with this support, Advay knew he could execute the payback, but one small hindrance remained. The only proof he had, thus far, of the involvement of Amar and the senior YSP members was his gut feeling. It was not enough to launch a full-fledged attack. He waited patiently to find some evidence, and eventually, he succeeded. He observed Amar leaving from college one day; he appeared very suspicious, constantly stared behind to ensure nobody followed him, and removed a large envelope from his bag. Advay carefully trailed him; his gut feeling once again spoke and told him he was on the right track to confirm his suspicions. Soon enough, Amar stopped at a shady alley and Advay took cover behind a large truck parked close by. A bike, of the same type that he had seen driving out of the campus, pulled up and stopped near Amar. A bulky and loud-mouthed man, who clearly looked like a goon demanded extra money since their gang had to suffer blows at the hands of the college students. Though Amar hastily signaled the man to talk at a lower volume, Advay had heard enough. He had his target in clear sight now.

The malicious alliance stuck together for a few days after the attack and tried their best to lay low, so as to not attract any unwanted attention. Advay went to college early the next morning and met with Ratan Singh's men. They waited silently for the opponents to come, and soon enough, a group of six boys led by Amar walked through the gates. Advay boldly stepped in front of them and from one look at his angry face and blazing eyes, they knew their secret had been uncovered.

"It seems you sent a few unwanted guests to my victory celebration," Advay coldly said. When they all stayed silent, he raised his voice and said, "There were girls there too. What if one of them had been hurt because of your stupidity? And how dare you harm my friends? You have a problem with me winning, take it up with me." With this, Advay landed a hard punch to Amar's flabby belly and he fell and rolled backward. Along with the two men sent by Ratan Singh, Advay made each of the boys accountable for every wound that his friends had sustained. But Advay knew this was not enough. He then grabbed Amar and one of the senior YSP members by their collar and dragged them near the main college building.

The news of the attack during Advay's party had spread like wildfire through the college. Ashish, Ravi, and the others had returned to college and every raw wound on their story conveyed the story of how severe the fight had been. The political rivalry had been more intense than ever that year, and like Advay, many people had drawn the obvious conclusion about who could be behind the attack. Hence, when they saw Advay with the two boys who looked like they had been beaten, they knew it was a sequel to that unfinished story. They gathered around to witness the events that would unfold. Advay saw his friends waiting near the classrooms. He made Amar and the other boy face them, and thundered, "Apologize to them." Nobody wanted to cross paths with this fierce and determined version of the usually calm and composed Advay. Not wanting to irk him further, the guilty boys hastily muttered a sorry to everyone they had hurt and scuttled away like a couple of scared mice.

Having successfully avenged his friends, Advay breathed a loud sigh of relief. Their college lives could now return to normal since he had made a loud, resounding, and clear declaration that nobody could hurt the people he cared about; not on his watch.

As everyone involved in the incident gradually recovered physically and mentally from its effects, Advay and his friends felt the heat of the third year and its demanding curriculum. It was a new obstacle, a higher mountain to scale, and a more formidable challenger than they had faced before. However, they were well-prepared to face it all. Advay and Ashish took it upon themselves to regularly plan study sessions for their group. They would discuss and revise concepts, solve complex problems together, and ensure that nobody felt burdened by the pressure of studies. While doing so, Advay had full-fledgedly embraced his title of General Secretary, and he made not only his friends and supporters, but his entire batch proud with his extraordinary work.

A fortnight later was Ashish's birthday. One evening, when the two had stayed back late in college to complete some extra studies, Advay asked him what he planned to do for the day. Ashish's cheeks went red; he absent-mindedly scratched his head, looked down, and hurriedly announced, "Nothing too special. Just that, I am planning to propose to Seema."

Advay was astounded, and happily yelled, "And that's nothing too special?!" Ashish grinned, and it was the first time that Advay had seen his friend so genuinely and purely happy about something. His eyes radiated a different kind of joy; the joy of anticipation of starting something new and beautiful. "To tell you the truth, I think it's the most special thing I have ever done!" Ashish confessed. "But, surely, it's the most difficult thing too. I know I want to do it, but I have no clue how to."

"What do you think I'm here for?" Advay asked while fondly slapping him on the back. "I'll help you plan it. It will be the most unique and surprising proposal ever!"

"I got the idea from something you had said during your birthday," Ashish continued. "I wanted to mark the day with a memory that would stay with me forever." Advay smiled, and they immediately started thinking of ideas.

A couple of days later, their plan was ready. Ashish wanted to pop the question to Seema at an amazing location, and he thought their joy would be increased even further if they could share it with all their close friends. Hence, he decided to host a party at one of the most lavish hotels in their city, Hotel Grand. He would invite a group of roughly twenty-five of their closest friends to partake in the dual celebration that would occur on that day.

Meanwhile, the responsibility of chauffeuring Seema to the location was entrusted to Advay. "Sure thing. I will get her there right on time!" Advay said. "Thanks," Ashish said, "But I also need you to do something else for me. You're going to tell her en route that I plan on proposing to her."

Advay was baffled by why Ashish wanted him to ruin the surprise. "I think it might be too much of a surprise for her," Ashish said with a nervous smile. "She will come thinking that it's a normal birthday party, and suddenly I'll be going down on a knee and proposing to her in front of so many people. The shock might make her say no," Ashish tried to joke, but Advay could see that even the idea of her refusing made him very nervous.

"Okay, okay; I completely understand," he said, his tone a blend of reassurance and mischief. "I'll break the news in the most subtle manner to keep up the required surprise," Advay reassured his friend.

"Thank you," Ashish told Advay, a warm and relieved smile spreading over his face. "I think with all your help, it's going to turn out to be one of the best days of my life!"

Advay smiled back and advised Ashish to let go of his nervousness and enjoy the days leading up to it. As he walked back home that evening, he reflected on how differently the dynamics of his life and relationships could have shaped up over the past two years. He remembered the butterflies he had felt in his stomach on the very first day that he saw and spoke with Seema. However, once he had given Ashish his word that he would not pursue her any further, it had been fairly easy for him to abandon the possibilities of what could have happened out of regard for this friend, whom he had almost come to think of as a brother.

His mother always told him that whatever happened was for the best. He smiled as he thought about the happiness that would soon surge into the lives of two people whom he considered his cherished friends, and believed that fate had shaped every incident that had led up to this day for a very good reason.

Chapter 7: Friendship, Love & Entangled Emotions

All the secret plans, preparations, and teeming excitement culminated in the arrival of Ashish's birthday.

Inexplicably, Advay had a very strange gut feeling that was gnawing his insides. Though he was usually very astute in recognizing his thoughts and emotions, he just could not categorize these. Granted, that it was a big day for his friend and he wanted everything to go smoothly. However, it did not explain the anxious jitters and that tingly sensation spreading throughout his being. He grappled with some possible explanations, but came up empty-handed each time.

The party was due to start at six. Seema's hostel was almost an hour away from the venue and hence, Advay left home early in the evening to ensure that he did not reach late and delay Ashish's plans. He had taken the whole day to calm himself and as he set out, he was determined to shut out every nagging feeling or thought that kept him from being fully focussed on his friend's happiness. He reached her hostel gate, and saw that she was already waiting for him, waving her hand toward him happily.

"Hi! I was very pleasantly surprised when you offered to pick me up. Did you get a new bike?" she inquired.

"No, I borrowed it from Ravi for today," Advay replied.

"I'm glad you did. And by the way, you look very nice today. This black shirt really suits you," Seema smiled and told him.

Advay gazed at Seema and realized that she was, in fact, the one worthy of all compliments for her appearance. She had on a long black skirt that perfectly complimented her height and a bright pink top that made her look livelier than ever. Her wavy hair was tied back in an elegant braid that emphasized her delicate features. Advay shyly thanked her for her compliment and hastily said, "You look really nice too." She flashed him a dazzling smile and took her place behind him.

Hearing her cheerful voice and melodious laugh took Advay's mind away from his disoriented feelings of the whole day. Shortly later, Advay thought of sharing with her the details of the grand surprise that was in store for her. "I need to tell you something," he said, partially looking back at her.

He heard her emit a soft sigh, after which she snuggled closer to him on the seat and tenderly held his shoulders, which sparked Advay's body with an electrifying sensation. She replied, "Me too. But not like this, where I can barely hear or see you. Why don't we stop somewhere? We will still reach on time."

Advay nodded and decided to halt at a small restaurant just a few meters further along the way. They made their way to a table and before she could say anything, Advay ordered tea for himself and a cup of strong coffee for her, which he knew was her favorite drink. Seema felt elated that he remembered that small detail about her; she eagerly asked him, "What did you want to tell me?"

Advay took a deep breath, steadying himself against some undercurrents that he could not quite explain, and said, "Ashish is going to propose to you today at the party." He was shocked to see the expression that etched itself on Seema's face.

She looked deeply troubled and disturbed, and before he could react, she let out a small yelp, "No! This can't be happening!"

Advay was taken aback. He had anticipated her to act shy, get nervous or flustered, but this reaction had come completely out of the blue. He was no expert in reading the emotions of girls, but it was clear that the news had not made Seema remotely happy or excited.

Advay hastily leaped to her side to salvage the situation. He awkwardly tapped her shoulder, and said, "It's okay to be nervous! It's a very big moment in your life."

"I'm not nervous," she shot back immediately. "I am upset, because I am in love with you. I have been since a while."

Her words made Advay's mind go numb. She was staring intensely at him after confessing her feelings. He found it hard to keep meeting her gaze and yet, he could not look away. Seema had made a special place in his heart right from their first interaction on the volleyball court. However, the bond of brotherhood shared between him and Ashish had made him bury those erupting feelings right then and there, and he had never permitted himself to bring them to the surface. Now, however, hearing Seema's side had changed the entire situation. Unknowingly and unwittingly, he was in the way of his friend's happiness. And the worst part of all this was that Seema had opened up the floodgates of those emotions that he had kept suppressed. He finally understood what his gut feelings were trying to tell him all day; as hard as he had tried for it to happen, he had not been able to see Seema as just a friend.

Her voice chimed out among the turmoil of his thoughts. "I have always had feelings for you; I was just waiting for the right time to tell you. Ashish is a dear friend, but he can be nothing more than that."

Advay was speechless; nothing made sense to him anymore. Seema too looked highly distraught and said in a small voice, "I think it's best if I don't come today. Tell Ashish I am not feeling well."

Advay wildly shook his head and tried to persuade her, "No, please; just come to the party. He has been so excited about this. It will ruin his day."

Seema continued with her valid argument that while she respected Ashish's feelings and efforts, she did not share them, and therefore, her presence at the party would only exacerbate the situation. Advay however, insisted that she should accompany him.

"Fine," she said. "But I have one request from you. You are going to tell Ashish the truth." Advay nervously gulped down upon hearing the condition she set forth, but eventually agreed. They left in a daze, with a thick cloud of discomfort, unease, and silence settling over them.

As they approached the venue, they spotted Ashish waiting out for them. He looked over Seema's shoulder and tried to ask Advay with subtle hand and eye gestures whether everything had gone smoothly. It was not a conversation that Advay could have in front of Seema, and hence, he tried to indicate that he would tell Ashish later. The three of them made their way toward the large hall, when Seema suddenly said that she needed to freshen up. She walked away and Advay saw his chance.

"I don't think you should do it today," Advay urgently told Ashish. As expected, Ashish's face fell, and he looked distraught. "Why, what did she say?" he inquired. Advay knew this was not the right time or place to reveal the complete story to Ashish; all that mattered now was stopping the proposal.

He hastily said, "She got very shy at the idea of being proposed to in front of so many people." Ashish's shoulders, which were tensed up, suddenly dropped in relaxation. "If that is the issue, I'll just do it after everyone leaves. It will be an intimate and private thing," he happily said.

Panic swirled in Advay's mind and he suddenly blurted out, "No, it's not just that." Ashish's eyes narrowed and he asked, "What do you mean?" Advay tried hard to create another plausible explanation and said, "She wants to focus on her studies." He knew the minute the words escaped his mouth that he had messed up. Both his fake excuses did not align with one another, and rightly so, it raised suspicion in Ashish's mind. He was evidently upset and confused, for his meticulous plan seemed to be getting ruined for reasons beyond his understanding.

'What exactly did you both talk about?" Ashish asked him. "Tell me the truth, please. You know how important this is to me."

Precisely because he knew how important it was to Ashish, he could not simply spill out the reality. He needed to think about the best way to do it, for he knew that it could unravel many negative emotions of hurt, betrayal, anger, and mistrust among them.

"Say something!" Ashish cried out. But just then, their other friends arrived and Advay heaved a sigh of relief. Soon, the grand hall was filled with guests. Advay, Ashish, and Seema stayed in opposite corners of the room. On the face of it, they seemed like they were enjoying as much as everyone else was. In reality, however, they were lost in a ferocious whirlwind of discomforting thoughts.

Shortly after the cake-cutting was done, Seema took Ashish aside and said that she wanted to go back. "But it's barely nine o'clock!" he said, looking terribly upset. "It was a wonderful party, but I really have to leave," she said with a smile, for she did not want to hurt him any more than she already had.

"Can you please wait for some time? Once everyone leaves, I will drop you." Seema hesitated, for she was afraid that Ashish would act on his plans while dropping her back. She chose her words carefully, and said, "It's your birthday today, you should not be driving around the city. I will ask Advay instead since it is on the way for him."

Ashish's face took on a stony expression, but he did not say anything. "Sure, if that's what you will prefer," he curtly replied.

Advay found Seema waiting outside, and they quietly walked ahead. Seema eventually asked, "Did you tell him everything?" "No," Advay immediately replied. "I had already ruined his party; I couldn't ruin his day further with the truth."

Seema remained quiet for a few moments and then replied, "I understand. And I am sorry for the part I played in it. I put you in an uncomfortable spot; but all I wanted to do was express what was in my heart. And I hoped…," she started saying but broke off without completing the statement.

Advay heard the words that she refused to speak. He wished dearly that he could openly reciprocate her feelings. He wished that they had not been caught in this intricate web spun by the ties of love and friendship.

Once he reached home, he silently opened the door and went to his room. He sank into his bed and surrendered to the quiet and dark.

"Ashish loves Seema…. But Seema loves me…and I…" The thoughts kept reiterating, but he could not get himself to confess his true stand on the matter even in his own mind. Either way that he looked at it, he felt he was wrong.

When he thought about Ashish, guilt threatened to consume him. It would be very hard to explain the unfortunate nature of the events that had folded, for Ashish would rightly think that Advay had continued to pursue Seema despite giving Ashish his word that he would not.

When he thought about Seema, he felt cornered. She was not wrong in voicing out her feelings, nor was she wrong in going against the decision that Advay and Ashish had made amongst themselves. He was so caught up that whole evening in fixing things with Ashish that he had never stopped to think how emotionally distressing the evening would have been for her.

He sat in silent contemplation for a long time and after a few hours, he made his decision. The first step ahead for him was coming clean to Ashish about everything. And the second was to break off contact with Seema; he did not see any way that they could go back to being friends, neither was there a way for them to become anything more than friends. His loyalty to Ashish would not permit him to do so. He could not see any way to restore the beautiful bond they all had shared. All he could do now was to prevent things from worsening.

The next day when Advay found Ashish alone for a minute, he sidled up to him and frantically said, "I need to talk to you." Ashish merely grunted in acknowledgment and slumped into a chair at the canteen. "I'm sorry I let you down yesterday. You trusted me with something very important, and I could not come through for you," Advay said. "You deserve to know why your special day was spoiled," he declared and went on to reveal the events that had unfolded the previous day.

A stony silence settled between them, and when Ashish eventually spoke, Advay's worst fear materialized. "I openly talked about this with you a long time ago. If this was what you wanted, why didn't you just tell me then?"

Ashish ignored Advay's repeated insistence that he had never pursued Seema and that he had no idea till yesterday about how she felt. "I just wish you had told me earlier. I thought we were friends," Ashish spat out. Advay's words were falling on deaf ears for Ashish refused to believe that Advay too was caught as unaware in the whole scenario as he was.

"I don't expect you to believe me right away. But I just need you to know that I am going to completely cut off contact with Seema. I don't want to cause any more damage than I have."

Before Ashish could respond, they heard a voice next to them say, "How kind of you to tell me this big decision that you've made about me."

Seema was standing there; her eyes reflecting immense anger and hurt.

"Whatever may be going on between the two of you, I don't deserve to be treated this way. You cannot decide between yourselves who I should develop feelings for," she said. Advay and Ashish exchanged a shocked glance amongst themselves which she noticed, and said, "Yes, I heard all that. And it was enough for me to know that I don't want to be part of this anymore." She turned on her heel and quickly left.

It felt like another fierce blow was dealt to Advay. He thought of going behind her to clarify things but instantaneously thought about how Ashish would take it. He was, literally, torn between the two of them.

Eventually, he stayed back and tried to talk to Ashish, but to no avail. Ashish too got up and said, "I never expected you to do this. Just stay away from me," he said and walked off. Advay was left all alone, with a gaping chasm in his heart caused by the loss of two very important people in his life.

He did not remember how he made his way home. He felt disoriented and disengaged from reality. His legs felt weak and his senses were numbed; despite his desperate efforts to salvage both these relationships, he had rendered them in a worse state than before. Advay shut himself in his room; he did not know how many hours passed by, when a knock sounded on his door.

"Come out, Advay. Tell me what is troubling you," said Sridevi's comforting voice.

He emerged from the room, and poured his heart out to her. Her calmness helped his raging thoughts to focus. She slowly said, "This is a tricky one, because all of you are right in your own way."

"Just tell me what I should do," Advay said in a small voice. "I tried to handle things my way, but I made everything worse." She talked him out of the downward spiral of his thoughts. "You cannot control how they will react, or whether they will believe you, so don't even try to control it. All you can do is stay true to yourself and allow them the opportunity to ponder over everything. I am sure things will fall in place."

He suddenly felt relaxed. Even when it seemed like a lost cause, his mother had shown him hope. Over the next few days, whenever worry and sorrow threatened to engulf him, he remembered his mother's words. He could not, and hence should not try to control Ashish and Seema's reactions. All he could do was wish and pray for things to fall back into place, which he fervently did.

His wait finally ended after two long months. As he approached his home one day, he saw some people sitting in the living room from the window. They had their backs to him, but he knew exactly who it was. Their voices were achingly familiar, and he had been craving to hear them.

He rushed in and opened the door to see Ashish and Seema enjoying a cup of tea with his mother.

As happy as he was, Advay was too stunned to speak. Memories of his last encounters with both of them came to his mind. Their eyes had shown nothing but anger and hurt against him, and their words had pierced his heart like sharp daggers. Today, however, it felt different.

Ashish looked him squarely in the face, got up, and pulled him into a hug. He could feel the distrust and misunderstanding fade away between them, and he felt joy coursing through him. He then turned to Seema, who smiled at him with the same warmth that she always radiated.

They ventured to Advay's room and as soon as he shut the door behind them, Ashish declared, "I'm really sorry. I acted terribly." He gulped hard and continued saying, "I was just too confused, upset, and angry about the situation. And it all came out on you. I accused you of horrible and untrue things, and just refused to see the truth. But finally, sense came knocking to my doorstep, and so, here I am," he said and gave a tentative grin.

Advay smiled back, and they nodded their heads at each other which wordlessly communicated that their differences had been resolved.

Ashish & Seema stayed back for a while and the trio light-heartedly exchanged stories and fun gossip, without any traces of awkwardness in the air. Then, he subtly pulled Advay aside and said, "I know this is great fun, but do you intend for the three of us to sit talking together the whole time?" Advay looked confused to which Ashish jokingly said, "You're so naïve, my friend. Talk to Seema! Tell her how you truly feel."

Just then, Seema went out to get a glass of water, unaware of the hushed conversation that was taking place. Advay's face went red upon hearing Ashish's comment and he abruptly mumbled, "I don't feel anything; we're just friends."

Ashish stared at him intensely and said, "You've proved your loyalty to me by offering to break off contact with her for my sake. But now, it's my turn to be a solid friend. I cannot let you abandon your feelings. She is a wonderful girl, and she deeply cares about you. In fact, she's the one who eventually brought me to my senses. I thought of talking with her first before coming to you, and she calmly sat me down and explained everything. She has forgotten her rightful anger against both of us. She really is perfect. Nothing will make me happier than to see my best friend have someone like that in his life."

Advay was so touched and grateful that he could not respond for many seconds. He eventually confessed to Ashish that he had strong feelings for Seema, but he had never considered it out of regard for Ashish. The latter nodded solemnly and said, "I was stupid for not believing that earlier. But I do now. I know what you were willing to sacrifice for me, and I won't at all have it. I'm going to leave now. You're going to talk to her and give me a big treat later to celebrate."

The door swung open, and in walked Seema. Even in a simple and casual look, she managed to take Advay's breath away. Without wasting a second, Ashish said he needed to leave, and on his way out, gave a mischievous and meaningful look to Advay. Seema caught it too, and once they were alone, she cocked an eyebrow at Advay and teasingly asked, "So, do you have something to say to me?"

Advay gently took her hand, and nodded. "I have so many things to tell you, if you will let me." She gave him a dazzling smile and they talked for hours after that. Advay took her back in time to when he had first laid sight on her, and how enamored he had been after their very first interaction. He profusely apologized once again for making a decision with Ashish on her behalf, but she gently interrupted him.

"I have forgiven you. That is all in the past now, and I don't want to look back. I want to look ahead, at what the future holds for you, me, and us."

They exchanged tender glances, and stayed a little longer in the euphoric bubble of their new and budding romance. Shortly later, Advay sensed that something was on Seema's mind. When he asked her, she said, "I know whatever happened between you and Roshni was a long time ago. I know you both have healthily moved on. But..." she said and faltered.

"But, what?" Advay inquired. "I know your career and ambitions are very important for you, as they are for me. And while I don't feel the same, I completely respect your fears that a relationship may distract you from your goals. I don't want you to resent me after a few years, or think badly about us," she said in a small voice and hung her head.

Advay placed his hand under her chin and made her look up at him. "You encourage me to do my best in everything, every single day. And I really mean this. Be it in volleyball, when I used to practice my hardest to come and show off in front of you, or during our group study sessions when I used to feel elated to answer your questions that nobody else could," he said and she chuckled softly in response.

"If you cannot push me toward my best, then nothing can. You're the biggest motivation and source of inspiration for me. I don't have anything to fear if I have you at my side."

And so, with a promise to care, cherish, and support one another through anything and everything, Advay and Seema embraced this beautiful form that their relationship had taken. In a mere matter of one day, Advay's life had fallen back into place and felt complete. The stars twinkled brighter for him that night and the moon seemed to emit an even prettier light than usual, for the most important people in his life had returned to him, and their bonds were now stronger than ever.

Chapter 8: Treading New Paths

The soft glow and radiance of his blossoming love cast a bright halo around Advay. It felt like a missing piece from the puzzle of his life had seamlessly fit in and completed a beautiful picture.

The fourth year of engineering introduces a notoriously challenging period in the life of every student who had to face it. Advay and Seema made a pact to cherish every moment before college resumed. They strolled through local parks, sharing laughter and secrets under the comforting shade of trees they had planted together. Exploring scenic spots in their city, they reveled in each other's company, knowing that their leisurely hours of spending time together would soon become scarce.

Two days before the start of their college, Advay decided to share the news about Seema and himself with his family. When he brought Seema home the next morning, Sridevi greeted them with a warm smile and ushered them in. Seema, who was usually very free and comfortable talking to Sridevi, was extremely nervous and quiet. Advay and Seema quietly took their place on opposite ends of a sofa and exchanged awkward glances every few seconds.

"I have not seen you in so long, beta! How have you been?" Sridevi inquired.

Seema quickly replied, "I'm sorry about that Aunty. I was very caught up in my studies and volleyball practice. I am good, I hope you're doing well too."

They talked for a few minutes and Advay could sense Seema's growing anticipation as the moment of the big reveal kept getting delayed. He knew he had to lead the conversation and was busy finding the right words for it.

Just then, Sridevi asked, "Where are your other friends? I was expecting them all."

Advay knew he had to act fast now, because Sridevi was under the assumption that his plan to bring Seema home was nothing out of the ordinary. He cleared his throat and hastily said, "I didn't call them, because they are not needed here. I specially got Seema home to tell you that I like her."

Seema felt her face reddening; she got very shy and lowered her gaze. Sridevi, on the other hand, appeared puzzled. "I also really like her, she's so lovely, smart, and well-mannered. What is so special that you thought of telling me this now?" she quizzically asked.

Advay let out a soft grunt, sensing that the conversation was veering away from where he intended it to go. The thought of revealing his profound emotions to his mother made him uneasy; Seema was not just someone he cared for deeply, she was his everything. Yet, his gentle efforts to express the significance of their bond seemed futile. Caught in a dilemma, he was on the verge of speaking out when Sridevi's quiet laughter reached his ears.

"I was just teasing you both. As a mother, I know when something is going on with my son. Are you both in love?"

Advay and Seema's heads shot up in unison. They found Sridevi looking at them with a smile and a glint in her eyes over their utterly shocked expression. "I put two and two together after Seema and Ashish's visit that day, the lengthy stay in your room, and Ashish's early departure. I was hoping that you both would sort out all the misunderstandings of your bad phase, and given how happy Advay looked after that, I realized it had happened. And I got the final hint yesterday, when he said that he was bringing you home. I realized that it was not merely his friend Seema coming to meet me, but someone who was very important to him."

When the young couple confessed the truth, Sridevi looked elated. She walked up to Seema and gave her a loving hug and a kiss on her forehead. "I wholeheartedly approve of this match, and I will support all the decisions you both make," she said. However, her demeanor quickly shifted to a serious one. "That being said, right now, your priorities need to be elsewhere. The final year of college is just the start of a long journey ahead. You should not let this distract you from the responsibilities of your academic and professional pursuits."

They assured her, and themselves, that their relationship would never come in the way of their studies and subsequent professional endeavors. They vowed to become each other's strengths and not weaknesses through everything that would come in the days ahead.

Right from day one of the fourth year, Advay was caught in a whirlwind of things that needed his focus. Academically, his attention and learning capacity were pushed to the brink. Regular internal assessments and submissions left no room for slacking. Politically, he was chosen to run for the post of President. Driven by loyalty to his party and supporters, he campaigned tirelessly and secured a resounding victory.

Advay Varma's name was etched in gold in the college's history, having won every election he stood for over the past four years.

As President, Advay had a mountain of responsibilities thrust upon his shoulders. Since he had been a dutiful and efficient office-bearer in the past, he wanted to live up to his own legacy and end his streak in a blaze of glory. He dedicated himself to fulfilling the expectations set for him, while ensuring that he did well in his academics. In the meanwhile, as time passed by, the upcoming Graduate Aptitude Test in Engineering (GATE) became one of the most prominent talking points for his friends and batchmates. It was an exam to open doors to postgraduate programs for engineering students. Advay, who scarcely kept track of time amidst his academic and extracurricular engagements, had decided against attempting it that year since he had not had the time to prepare. It was thus to his immense surprise that a hall ticket for him for the exam arrived at his doorstep.

"It must be some kind of a mistake," Advay said to his parents, shaking his head in disbelief.

"There's no mistake," Sridevi intervened and Advay turned an astonished gaze at his mother. "I knew how busy you were, and that you felt underconfident to apply. But I have complete faith in your abilities, and so I requested Ashish to fill a form for you."

Advay felt immense distress as the exam was only two weeks away, and this unexpected development had caught him off guard. He contemplated seeking Ashish's advice. Despite his annoyance at Ashish for keeping him uninformed, Advay honestly expressed his fear of being unprepared for the exam. Ashish wisely responded, "Consider it a challenging experience, and don't dwell too much on the outcome. You believe you're underprepared, but in reality, you've diligently studied the same concepts. Trust yourself—it's all in your mind." Encouraged by Ashish's words, Advay decided to bet on his own abilities. In the time that he had left, Advay immersed himself in preparation. If not for himself, he wanted to do it for Sridevi, who trusted him even when he could not trust himself.

As he walked into the exam center, Advay soothed his anxiety by reassuring himself that the very worst outcome of the test would also not put him in any different position from where he had originally planned to be. With these liberating thoughts, his mind was freed from the shackles of inhibition and self-doubt and he entered the hall with a tranquil positivity spreading through his mind. As Ashish had correctly foreseen, the questions did not seem as alien to Advay as he had feared. True to his nature, he poured every ounce of effort into tackling them, approaching each question with determination and intellect. Regardless of the results, he took pride in his diligence and exited the examination hall with a sense of accomplishment, his head held high.

A few weeks later, on the day of Advay's birthday, he and his friends were sitting in their college canteen and were engrossed in an exciting discussion about the celebration plans. One of their batchmates ran towards them and breathlessly announced, "The GATE results are up!" The final year students in the canteen broke out in a cacophony of excited and nervous squeals, animated chatter, and nervous speculations about what the results would display.

Ashish, Ravi, and all the others who had appeared for the exam immediately broke away from the group and raced ahead to the central lobby of the college where the results were displayed. Advay, however, stayed behind with the others. Although the exam turned out to be better than anticipated, he held no expectations of being selected for he knew that he had appeared unprepared.

The word quickly spread to the canteen that students, including Ashish, Ravi, and Samir, had made it onto the prestigious list. Advay's group was ecstatic, and they decided to merge the day's two joyous events into one grand festivity. As Ravi and the others triumphantly returned to the canteen, Advay realized Ashish was missing. Inquiring about his absence, the group began to search for him. Just then, they spotted Ashish sprinting towards the canteen, his face alight with happiness.

He made a beeline for Advay and burst out with excitement, "Now the celebration is truly complete! You've passed the exam as well, my friend!"

Advay looked at Ashish, his expression one of stunned silence, as he struggled to process the incredible news.

Ashish grinned and gave his shoulder a hearty pat. "All the others had already looked up their results, and each roll number had a corresponding name next to it. There was a single number left unclaimed, and upon closer scrutiny, I had a hunch it might be yours. That's why I headed to your house to grab your hall ticket for confirmation. Guess what, you've done it, my friend! Advay, you've set yet another benchmark for yourself as the only College President to have passed this prestigious examination."

Advay was in disbelief, his face breaking into a silly smile as he snatched up his hall ticket and dashed off to verify the results for himself. Ashish, Ravi & others followed him. Seeing his roll number on the list sent waves of happiness pulsing through him, echoing the exuberant rhythm of his heart. Overwhelmed with emotion, Advay embraced Ashish and the rest of the group in a warm hug.

That evening, Advay's home, adorned by Seema and Roshni, became the venue for the most spirited celebration of both Advay's birthday and his GATE exam triumph. The whole group, poised to set off on their individual paths, realized this might be one of their final chances to relish the joy of togetherness. Amidst the laughter, dancing, and chatter, they forged innumerable memories, creating bonds that would hold them together, no matter where life took them.

After crossing this momentous milestone and securing the best outcome possible from it, the next challenge was lined up for Advay. The season of campus placements would soon begin. It was the first and most significant opportunity for students to break out of the cocoon of college life and take a step toward venturing into the professional landscape. Advay knew that getting selected in placements meant winning half the battle; all he needed to do was pass the college exams, which he had meticulously worked for, and he would have a job ready for him. Since he had never previously planned to appear for the GATE, his vision for his future had entailed finding a good job after college. While he was overjoyed about the opportunities that passing the exam had opened up for him, he still wanted to weigh his options.

When the campus interviews rolled around, Advay's peers buzzed with nervous excitement, but he remained composed, his mind already racing ahead, envisioning his future. His first interview was with Tata Consultancy. As he entered the interview room, his calm confidence radiated, catching the attention of the recruiters. With each question posed to him, Advay's responses were nothing short of extraordinary. His insightful solutions to complex engineering problems left the interviewers in awe. It was as if he had a natural knack for unraveling the most intricate challenges with ease. His knowledge wasn't just confined to textbooks; Advay possessed a depth of understanding that transcended the classroom. He spoke passionately about his projects, demonstrating a practical approach that impressed even the most seasoned professionals in the room. He left the interview with an offer letter in his hand. Soon after, as his remarkable ascent in all interviews soared to new heights, he was also selected for attractive and lucrative positions in Lloyd Steels and Western India Limited.

Advay's reputation swiftly rose to prominence on campus. News of the extraordinary student predestined for success spread rapidly. This further cemented his status as an exceptional student, affirming the widespread belief: The entire college echoed with the sentiment that Advay was indeed a fortunate 'Owl'.

Shortly later, he found himself at the final threshold that he needed to cross before stepping into an exciting new world full of opportunities. As he walked into the familiar halls to sit for his final year assessment, a mixture of emotions flooded him. Nervousness at the exam itself, happiness at successfully completing his graduation, and a deep sorrow at leaving behind the place and the people who had made the past four years of his life magical. As each day went by, he put his heart and soul into reproducing the knowledge he had gleaned over the years onto the blank sheets of paper; he wanted them to be a testament to his thorough learning. And that's exactly what the papers worked as. Advay went on to become the highest scorer of his batch for two subjects and passed with flying colors in all the others. The consistent upward trajectory he upheld throughout the course reached its zenith at the end.

And now, Advay had a momentous decision to make. His own thoughts were in turmoil, unsure of which way to lead him. The advice that he solicited from others only deepened his confusion, for strong arguments were presented in favor of both his options. Pursuing a postgraduate degree would, undoubtedly, place him in the top rung of highly qualified engineers, which would help him secure an excellent job. However, there was also a lot to achieve by taking up the offers he had right now and gaining work experience in esteemed institutions. The path he chose now would significantly impact his life, and it was not a decision to be made in haste. He discussed in-depth with Seema and Ashish, who had each chosen to pursue different paths. Seema accepted an excellent trainee assignment at Wipro, a reputed firm in Pune, convinced that hands-on experience would serve as a more effective educator than pursuing further academic courses. Following his impressive performance in the GATE examination, Ashish opted to enrol in the Master of Technology program at IIT Delhi. He sought deeper learning and wanted to enjoy the experience of being a student for a while more.

Both these reasonings resonated deeply with Advay, making the task all the more difficult. He contemplated it for several days, but his internal debates did not seem to be ending. Eventually, he decided to trust his gut feeling; one that was strongly telling him to pursue his education further. He was drawn toward IIT Mumbai due to its proximity to Pune, as he wished to stay closer to Seema.

His parents supported his decision, as did Seema. Although it was Mumbai, their relationship was set to meet its first challenge- the many miles that would now separate them. However, they both were empowered by their immense affection and undying faith in one another; they would tackle this challenge too and ensure that their love would prevail over all. Moving away from his family too was difficult, but their excitement at the new journey he was embarking upon made it much easier. From his father, Advay got a pat on his back and a gruff confession of how proud he had made him. His mother, always strong and composed, kept a smiling face while blessing him but the tears in her eyes conveyed the emotions she held back. His sister, juggling the sorrow of Advay going away and happiness at the wonderful opportunity he had got, hugged him tightly and gave him a frame of a beautiful family photograph. Their love, good wishes, and fond memories became his companions and he treaded a new and unfamiliar path.

The Indian Institute of Technology at Mumbai was every bit as impressive as the stories had described it to be. While the infrastructure and the enormous area that the campus covered were amazing, it was the sheer aura of it that left the most lasting impact. It was more than just a college; it was a legacy of brilliance, and Advay felt incredibly humbled to be a part of it.

Advay was pleased to have his classmate Samir join him in the same college, yet he couldn't help but miss the camaraderie that he shared with his group back home. Nevertheless, he soon made new friends. He befriended Aarti Barve, who was a senior in charge of managing the student body as well as the other facilities of the college like the mess, recreational zone, sports arena, etc. They bonded over their political acumen, and she was impressed with Advay's feats. She encouraged him to try his hand at student politics there too, and advised that the Post Graduate Representative would be an ideal position for him.

"You're responsible, proactive, and a very composed person," she explained. "You're tailor-made for it because it needs someone who can strongly represent the interests of other students."

Advay had always been drawn toward the idea of helping others and lending them a voice when they could not speak for themselves. His sincerity for the cause was evident from the way he talked and worked with others, and he quickly won their trust. He embraced all the responsibilities that came with his new leadership position. He conducted and attended regular discussions, struck a good working relationship with the other office bearers through integrity and honesty, and proved himself as a worthy choice for the post.

Additionally, he was assigned the task of managing the college mess. He knew that most of the students, like him, craved the comfort of home food and was determined to make the mess good enough to make this transition a little easier for everyone. He conducted surveys to learn what the students wanted, and simultaneously coordinated with the cooks to understand if they faced any difficulties. He knew that clear communication could improve any status quo and tried to use the same approach. His efforts paid off over time; students would come up to him and thank him for improving their food experience, and likewise, the cooks too expressed their happiness at some of the changes he had suggested in their practices. He was elated, but there was already a new complication waiting for him. A group of local, senior students were notorious for delaying the payment of their dues. The amount was fairly large, and it disrupted the smooth functioning that Advay had worked hard to achieve. Advay tried reasoning with them, but he received dismissive answers. He endeavoured to devise a creative strategy, and ultimately, he formulated the perfect solution.

He crafted sizable banners and displayed them throughout the campus, showcasing his reward and penalty system. He publicly called out those who were behind on payments by affixing their names to the bulletin boards. Additionally, he instructed the cafeteria servers to deny service to these individuals. Moreover, he acknowledged those who settled their bills promptly with free confectionery, while also introducing a policy that made the late payers responsible for the cost of these treats. His approach was clever; it served both as a preventive measure and a motivator. In just a short span, the mess's financial records were completely sorted. Advay had not only addressed a persistent issue but also implemented a solution to prevent its recurrence.

Advay quickly carved a place for himself within the social echelons of his new college. Everyone was already fascinated by the dynamic student who had excelled in the position of Post Graduate Representative, and his warmth and sincerity while interacting with others only made him more popular. His peers regarded him as a smart, witty, charming, and helpful person who could be approached for any problem big or small. Unwittingly, he captured the hearts of many of his female classmates and, much to their chagrin, proudly told them about Seema whenever they probingly asked about his personal life.

In addition to his extracurricular and social activities, he also excelled academically. Although the curriculum and instructional methods were unfamiliar to him, he adapted and integrated as effortlessly as a chameleon camouflage with its surroundings. An intriguing aspect of his program required Advay to instruct B-Tech students. Without any previous teaching background, he discovered a natural talent for it. The students reacted with great enthusiasm and engagement to his teaching style, making his sessions the most dynamic and participatory.

"I might land in trouble for saying this out loud, but I believe your teaching surpasses even that of some professors," Deepak, a dedicated and earnest B-Tech student, confided.

Advay's response was a warm smile, acknowledging the genuine compliment. His rapport with Deepak had grown over time, marked by Deepak's keen participation in every session Advay conducted. Advay had gained the admiration of his peers, and he found great joy in teaching, which was mirrored by the students' enthusiasm in learning. The faculty also took note of his potential. Through their experienced eyes, they recognized his distinct and resilient character.

One of the most significant aspects that IITs prided themselves on was their placements. Knowing that the halls of these institutes housed some of the sharpest and brightest minds, leading companies came flocking to their doors. This time around, the stakes were higher than before for Advay to secure a good job, for that was the obvious path that his career would follow. Or at least that's what Advay believed, as blissfully unaware as he was of the thrilling tale that his destiny had penned down for him.

Advay knew that his resume would be the first and informal introduction of him that any recruiter would have. It would be the foundation on which they would base their first impression of him. He knew that the attitude and mentality with which they evaluated him would be largely determined by that single piece of paper. It was the key that could open up doors of opportunity for him, or keep him shut away from professional growth and excellence. He put tremendous effort into creating the perfect resume. It was crisp, clear, and yet succinctly told the glorious tale of all his educational endeavors. He wanted it to be a self-portrait that, in all honesty, gave anyone who read an insight into his mind and personality. He included and elaborated on all the achievements that he prided himself on most. In the section that outlined his strengths, he candidly stated, "Never failed in any exam I have taken." He believed this was an important detail to include, reflecting his trust in his rational judgment.

On the inaugural day of placements, Advay had the luck of being shortlisted for Larsen & Toubro, a renowned firm with a global presence. Upon entering the hall, he exchanged pleasantries with the interviewers, deftly concealing the nervousness underlying this crucial interview, and summoned all the confidence he could muster. He was grilled with some of the most difficult and complex questions he had ever encountered. They tested his conceptual knowledge, practical skills, and analytical thinking abilities. Advay handled them better than most of the other interviewees, and his skills in the subject were highly commendable, the recruiter told him while appearing evidently impressed. At the very end, they asked Advay a question that, for the first time in the whole interview, baffled him momentarily.

"Is there any reason why we should not hire you?" the recruiter asked, and it was clear from the expression in his eyes that he had laid it out as an intriguing challenge for Advay. He was not looking for the typical and obvious answer, wherein one would vehemently deny the existence of any such reason and insist on how perfect they were for the role.

Advay thought of it for a second, for he was determined to end the interview on a good note. Slowly he said, "I mean no disrespect, but I am not aware of how your company works and what kind of hierarchy system it follows. I can learn to do anything needed from me, but I will not be able to become a brown-noser. I will not follow instructions that do not sit right with me simply because a superior has ordered them. I believe in open communication, where suggestions coming from everyone are equally valued and considered with an open mind. I cannot be a yes-man. If that is something required in the company culture, I humbly suggest that I not be considered."

The recruiter heard his answer and a slight smile curved on his lips. Their eyes flashed immense respect for Advay, which meant more to Advay than any verbal praise. The recruiters went aside, discussed amongst themselves, made a few calls, and returned to happily announce to Advay, "We would love to have you on board! Our new office in the United States needs someone exactly like you. You will receive an official offer letter within a few days."

Advay couldn't believe what he was hearing; that he had such an incredible opportunity in his hands. He battled to keep his euphoria under control and react in a professional and dignified manner. But soon after he left the room, he let out an overjoyed cry and jumped up while pounding his wrist in the air. He could not wait to share the news and discuss it with the people most important to him, for his life decisions did not solely impact him. He quickly shared the happy news with his family and Seema, and decided to take some time to introspect on the implications and possibilities that lay ahead of him if he accepted the job.

In the meantime, Advay's resume and his conduct during the interview became the talk of the college. Many final year B.Tech students approached him seeking guidance, advice, and interview tips, all of which Advay graciously provided. The college faculty also invited him to share his insights with senior students, a request Advay promptly accepted. During one of the sessions held for Deepak's class, at the conclusion of his talk, Advay noticed Deepak standing quietly with his hand raised.

Prompted by curiosity, Advay encouraged him to finish his thought. After a brief pause, Deepak continued, "You mentioned that you've never failed an exam. But I'm interested to know, have you ever faced an exceptionally challenging test and succeeded in that as well?"

Amused by the question, Advay told him about his exceptional performance in the 10th and 12th board exams, his consistent excellence during four years of engineering, and his success in the crucial GATE exam, as well as his selection in all four interviews he attended.

Yet, Advay observed Deepak nodding his head, indicating he wasn't particularly impressed by his narration.

Once Advay finished, Deepak interjected, "That's fine Sir, but I was referring to a challenging exam like the Staff Selection Board (SSB) interview for entry into the Indian Army. Do you think you can pass that too if you attempt it?"

Advay was completely taken aback by the direction that their conversation had veered to. He had heard that Deepak's father was in the Army, and following his father's footsteps was Deepak's strongest ambition. Deepak was preparing for the SSB interview, and had experienced firsthand how incredibly demanding it was. He hence broached the topic with Advay, whom he immensely respected, about whether Advay's claim in his resume could hold true for the SSB exam too. Unknowingly, he ignited a spark of a challenge for Advay.

Like every Indian citizen, Advay too had the highest regard for the military brave hearts who risked their lives for the wellbeing of others. However, he had never in his wildest imagination thought of joining Army forces & was clueless about SSB interview.

Deepak's words had stirred something within him. Granted, that his achievements so far had indeed been creditable. However, what greater validation would he get of his talents than by knowing that he was capable enough to join the army? It was the most difficult test he would ever undertake and determination to prove himself worthy, in his own eyes, flooded through every inch of his being.

He solemnly nodded and said to Deepak, "I can answer your question only after I attempt the exam. And that's exactly what I am going to do."

He had arrived at a decision that would completely transform his life as he knew it.

Chapter 9: Chronicles of Brilliance & Bravery

There was a stunned silence on the phone. Advay sighed softly; having received a similar reaction from his parents when he shared the news, he was prepared for Seema's response about his upcoming SSB interview.

When Seema finally found her voice, she slowly asked, "You have a job in hand from a great company, right? And now you are attempting the selection exam for the Indian Army? I don't understand..." and she trailed off again.

Advay explained the entire series of events that had led up to him taking this decision. He passionately told Seema that this was much more than a frivolous challenge that his junior had given him; it was the ultimate test that Advay could set for himself, and success in it would have much more meaningful implications than anything he had ever done before. He explained the fierce and burning desire that had ignited in him, and that it would consume him if he did not take up the challenge.

Seema, who could always read Advay's deepest emotions and thoughts, instantly understood and communicated her undying support for him. She knew how determined and tenacious he was, it was one of the qualities that she deeply admired about him, and she knew there was no stopping him now. He would move the heavens and earth if he needed to, but he would prepare as rigorously as he could and attempt the exam.

The first step ahead for Advay was understanding the structure and methodology of conduct of the 5-day SSB interview. Deepak, who was also surprised that Advay had taken his challenge so seriously, always had immense respect for Advay but it had increased multifold upon seeing Advay's grit and resolve. He helped Advay in whatever way he could. In the few weeks that he had at his disposal, Advay immersed himself in understanding the process.

Soon after, he and Deepak received their call letters, the gateway to joining the leagues of Army officers. Advay felt a rush of expectation as he gripped the letter, realizing the gravity of the moment. Leaving their college behind, Advay & Deepak embarked on a momentous journey—one that would alter Advay's life forever. With the blessings and support of loved ones, they stepped onto the train from Mumbai to Bhopal, their mind buzzing with anticipation for the challenges that lay ahead.

At the Bhopal railway station, they were received by Army personnel at a reception counter on the platform. Seeing the charisma they exuded and the respect their uniform commanded, Advay felt a shiver of exhilaration; would he too dawn it someday? The candidates, hailing from numerous states but united by a common vision, were organized into batches and escorted to the Army buses for the onward journey to the SSB center.

On the bus, Advay found himself seated next to a young man who gave him a quick glance and almost immediately asked whether it was Advay's first attempt.

"How did you know?" Advay asked, surprised.

The man, who introduced himself as Aseem, grinned and said, "Your hairstyle and stubble gave it away. Most of us frequent attempters have short, military-style cuts."

Aseem went on to reveal that it was his sixth attempt at the SSB, and Advay couldn't help but be amazed at his unwavering passion for the Army. He thought of using the bus ride to soak in the invaluable experiences that Aseem would have acquired over the years, and asked Aseem all the doubts that he still had about the grueling interview that he would face.

Upon arrival at the SSB center, the candidates eagerly awaited the completion of their documentation and barrack assignments. Within that one room, there was a myriad of emotions-nervousness, thrill, composure, and some utterly stoic. Advay, Deepak, and Aseem were all assigned to barrack number twenty-three. Advay quickly bonded with three other candidates; Sunil from Rajasthan, and Venky and Janardhan from Andhra Pradesh. Their easy-going attitudes provided a welcome contrast to the broody moods of most of the other candidates. Even Aseem, despite his serious intent, joined in their light-hearted discussions and plans to explore the city.

"We should do it after the second day, however," Aseem suggested, and grimly informed the others that the Screening Test would determine which of them would stay ahead. The fact that for some of them, the trip to Bhopal would be as short as it would be disheartening, suddenly jolted everyone into doubling down on their preparations. Advay, however, chose to discover the campus, soaking in its vastness and ambiance. The mess hall, with its grand dining setup, captivated him. He noticed a smaller table with fine crockery, where selected candidates from earlier batches, now undergoing medical tests, dined—a sign of the preferential treatment accorded to them.

As he continued his exploration, his curiosity got the better of him and he went over to the barracks of selected candidates. He was staring, awestruck, when a voice from behind suddenly interrupted his racing flow of thoughts.

"Can I help you?" a man asked, and Advay slowly turned behind, fully expecting to be chastised for being there.

However, he was pleasantly surprised to see a burly and tall man smiling politely at him. The man introduced himself as Kiran Rana. Upon hearing that Advay was to attempt the assessment for the first time, he kindly offered a comprehensive briefing on the SSB process. He sat Advay down and explained the intricacies of Stage One, which included the Officer Intelligence Rating (OIR) and the Picture Perception and Description Test (PPDT). Stage Two, spread over four days, included psychological tests, Group Testing Officer (GTO) tasks, and personal interviews.

"The psychological tests aim to reveal your true thoughts and behaviors," Kiran explained, detailing tests like the Thematic Apperception Test (TAT), Word Association Test (WAT), Situation Reaction Test (SRT), and Self-Description (SD). He explained that TAT involved crafting twelve stories based on images displayed sequentially, with thirty seconds to view each picture and four minutes to write a story. The final image would be blank, prompting candidates to write a story reflecting a significant personal experience or an inspiring tale. In WAT, participants had fifteen seconds to write their immediate thoughts upon seeing each of the sixty words. SRT required quick, instinctive responses to sixty different scenarios within thirty minutes. These exercises aimed to uncover the personality traits sought in officer candidates.

Advay thanked Kiran profusely for helping him understand the full extent and magnitude of the task that lay ahead for him. Despite the nervous ripples, Advay remained resolute and determined as he walked back to his barracks, ready to face the challenge.

Following the first day's Screening Test, the number of candidates was reduced from one hundred and twenty to just thirty. Advay, Aseem, and three others from their group advanced, but Deepak did not. It felt like a harsh blow to Advay. Deepak had been the guiding light that had placed him on this thrilling and rewarding path, and now, he would have to continue along alone. The sense of loss was tangible as Advay bid goodbye to Deepak and rushed to find a place of solitude to compose himself and cope with this unfortunate development. Aseem and another member of their group, Sunil, sensed Advay's disappointment and persuaded him to join them for the planned excursion into the city. They spent a pleasant time exploring the city, visiting the Excon temple, indulging in some window shopping, and enjoying a meal at Chawla's, a well-known local restaurant.

On their way back in a long-bodied tempo that was famous within Bhopal, they observed a fellow passenger keenly overhearing their conversation. Suddenly, the man asked Aseem if they were there for the SSB interview. He was inebriated and looked rather disheveled. The group was surprised, as their conversation had been general and did not specifically mention the SSB interview. When questioned about how he had guessed, the young man introduced himself as Javed, whose father worked as an orderly at the SSB Campus, and they lived in the 'Followers Quarters' within the campus. He claimed he could spot an Army enthusiast with just one glance. The group listened attentively to his stories of the SSB campus and the lives of Army officers, and asked him questions about campus life, which he answered with vivid detail, demonstrating his intimate knowledge of the institute. Upon arriving at their destination, Javed hesitantly extended his hand, asking Aseem to lend him fifty rupees. He promised Aseem that he would repay the amount the following day. However, before Aseem could retrieve the money from his pocket, Advay quietly said that Javed might use it to have more alcohol, which would neither do him nor the others around him any good. However, Advay also had immense empathy and hence assured Javed that he personally would give him the required money the next morning.

Javed accepted this with a smile and took a couple of steps to leave; however, he abruptly turned back to address the group.

"If you all don't mind, may I say something?" he hesitantly asked, and intrigued, the entire group encouraged him to speak.

He raised a bony finger and placed a penetrating stare upon Advay and said, "I am sure you all are equally capable, Sirs, but I am quite certain this man is going to get selected."

The group chuckled as Sunil humorously brushed off Javed's remark, jesting about how he was predicting success for someone who had declined to lend him money and ignored the one who had offered it.

Javed quietly responded, "It's not that. I have seen a lot of people transform into officers. They have something in them, a spark that

I can't describe, and he has it too. He is sharp and blunt, and his eyes look like they have the wisdom of the world, like a wise owl's."

A silence took over the group as they all looked at each other, and then at Advay. With Javed's words lingering in his mind, Advay walked back with endless possibilities swimming in his thoughts.

The next day brought the onset of the second stage of interviews. The thirty candidates were assigned chest numbers through a random draw, and split into three subgroups, each containing ten individuals. The first subgroup was lined up for interviews, the second for psychological assessments, and the third for Group Testing Officer (GTO) tasks. Upon finishing their assigned tests, each subgroup would rotate to the next set of tests. Advay & Aseem, with chest numbers thirteen and eighteen, formed a part of Group Two. Advay demonstrated exceptional performance throughout the various stages. During a group discussion, when chaos ensued as everyone tried to express their viewpoints all at once, Advay intervened and impressed everyone with his inherent leadership skills. His calm demeanor and effective strategies quickly earned the group's respect. In the Military Planning Exercise too he was unanimously chosen as the leader, and in the Command task, which entailed a leader selecting a team member for assistance. Almost everyone expressed a desire to have him by their side. These experiences solidified his reputation as a leader and team player.

The momentous five days that had triggered a volcano of anticipation in Advay's heart seemed to end much before their time was due. Before he had even realized, all the tasks had been concluded and the results were to be announced soon. Prior to that, on the final day, there was a 'Conference Leg' where each candidate had a brief meeting with the board members. During this conference, candidates were asked a few general questions. Its purpose was solely to determine whether to recommend a particular candidate for an officer position in the forces. Most, including Advay, exited within minutes, but Aseem and Sunil were inside for thirty to forty minutes, sparking whispers that they might be the chosen ones.

As the President walked into the room, pin-drop silence took over as the candidates awaited the announcement of their fates with bated breath. Shortly before he had walked in, however, the hall was abuzz with silent yet clearly audible guesses of chest numbers two and eighteen being selected, which belonged respectively to Sunil and Aseem. The President smiled and referencing these guesses, he said, "You all are partially right. Chest number eighteen is selected. But, along with that, it is someone who performed incredibly well in every test; it is chest number thirteen!"

Advay's legs wavered, but he steeled himself. The announcement of his number flooded him with immense relief and happiness. He had done it. He wished Deepak could be there with him to celebrate, and see that Advay's impeccable track record of never failing an exam that he attempted remained intact. The others heartily cheered for Advay and Aseem, though the slight moistness in their eyes conveyed the crushing sorrow they felt. The President addressed their pain, and in a heartfelt speech, conveyed how there are many ways to serve the nation and others, as long as one remained pure in their intentions. Every person who heard the speech was filled with profound determination and resolve to achieve great things in life that could make a true difference.

While the other candidates eventually left the campus to come back stronger and better for the next assessment, Advay and Aseem stayed for the extensive medical examinations over the next three days. Advay passed, but Aseem was disqualified due to a heart murmur. Advay felt a complex mix of elation at his own selection and sorrow as another one of his friends was leaving the path that they had all embarked together upon. As they parted to go their separate ways, they shook hands with a heavy heart knowing their paths had diverged but their friendship remained unbroken.

Having been selected into the Indian Army, and having a wonderful job opportunity that gave him a coveted ticket to go abroad, Advay had the most difficult decision to make. His family, Seema, and even Ashish, whom he updated about the exciting new developments in his life all wondered how Advay would choose between two such exceptional opportunities, and how he would make the choice. His parents nudged him toward taking the US job; they believed it would set him up for a life of success and growth, and they wanted only the very best for their son. Seema too was very scared about the idea of Advay joining the Army, for she knew it was a life full of sacrifices and hardships. Advay, out of consideration for their valid concerns, took many days to evaluate his options. However, somewhere deep down, his decision had already been made, and that is what he went forward with.

He could not articulate when exactly it had happened, but he had realized that an aristocratic job abroad would never give him even part of the immense satisfaction that being an Army officer would. Perhaps it was the atmosphere of the campus where people put everything on the line for a chance to serve their nation, or the actual interactions that he had with officers that inspired him to follow their footsteps. And since he had got a chance, something that very few and very worthy individuals only got, he was not about to give it up. With a heart full of hope and the good wishes of those he considered as pieces of his heart, he took a step toward transforming his life that landed him at the doorstep of the Indian Military Academy.

As the bus drove into the Indian Military Academy located at Dehradun, the campus he saw around him felt like a different universe to Advay. The magnificent infrastructure and lush greenery of the Academy lay before him like the opened pages of a new chapter in his life; it felt like the very trees were telling him stories of courage and discipline. Advay stepped off from the bus, casually carrying his duffel bag on his shoulder full of some personal belongings and countless expectations. The officers strode purposefully about, barking orders in firm, clear voices, and young cadets could be seen scattered across the field, each focused intently on a task that challenged them.

The initial days at the Academy were incredibly challenging. Rest was a luxury as cadets were woken by the shrill sound of abrupt orders. They faced rigorous military routines, including physical endurance, drills, weapon handling, tactical exercises, and academic instructions. These activities tested their mental and physical resilience, aiming to instill discipline, strategic thinking, and the ability to perform under pressure.

The physical fitness sessions were brutal. Advay struggled to catch his breath, feeling the intense burn in his muscles revealing his lesser fitness compared to the cadets he aimed to match. During his initial fitness test, he faltered; his mind and body failed to synchronize due to overwhelming exhaustion, resulting in scores below the Academy's standards.

Even though he was at his lowest point, Advay's unbreakable will shined like a blazing light. Hoping that his senior could give him a lifeline, he bravely approached the Company Sergeant Major (CSM) and requested his help to improve his physical endurance. The CMS looked at Advay, the fire of determination burning in his eyes though he was exhausted beyond measure, and agreed to help him; thus commenced the most intensive phase of Advay's training. It became a routine for them to have their sessions in the evening. As the lights dimmed on the academy grounds, Advay and the CSM would sit on the empty sports field. In the dull light of the ceiling lamps, the CSM taught Advay to go through a program of specific exercises that included calisthenics, runs, rope climbs, and multiple sets of varied exercises. Every session was more challenging than the previous one, leaving Advay completely exhausted and on the verge of collapse.

The CSM often emphasized, 'Your body is merely a tool; it's your mind that requires conquering.' His assertive tone carried a motivational undertone. Advay interpreted the pain in his body as a sign that discomfort was transforming into evidence of physical training. The once daunting challenges now felt manageable, and his endurance steadily improved. Gradually, the sense of inadequacy waned, replaced by a belief that he could achieve his dream of becoming a soldier. These late-night training sessions under the stars not only built his muscles but also fortified his soul and spirit. His movements became fluid, swift, and controlled, reflecting the rigorous physical development. Mental toughness accompanied this progress, enhancing both his performance on the field and in academics. Advay's newfound discipline and focus allowed him to grasp intricate elements of military training and tactics.

He reaped the benefits of his unwavering dedication to physical fitness during a novice boxing tournament at the Academy. His honed skills and strategic prowess transformed him into an outstanding boxer. In each match, he not only demonstrated strength and skill but also keenly analyzed his opponents' minds. Every blow he delivered was meticulously planned, leading him to victory against all his challengers.

His streak of exemplary performance went much beyond the boxing ring. Excelling in academics, he secured the top position in the entire Battalion. He became well-liked and respected by his peers, who had once dismissed him as a below-average candidate. His instructors also noticed the change in him and were pleased with his fast progress. His mettle led to his appointment as Junior Under Officer (JCO), and finally passing out from the Academy as a silver medalist.

Advay got commissioned into the Corps of Engineers and reported to the College of Military Engineers, Pune to undergo his Young Officers (YO's) course. Here, he reconnected with Seema and they made up for all the time they had lost, and conversations they had missed out upon while they were both abiding by the demands of the destinies that they had each chosen. Weekends found them exploring the Sahyadri hills, waking up to mist-clad mountains, or strolling through the vibrant city markets, hand in hand, planning their future. Seema proved to be a stabilizing force in Advay's life and helped him find solace amidst the hustle and bustle of his training course. He deftly balanced his personal and professional commitments, completing his YO's Course with flying colors.

As his course drew to a close, it was time to leave Seema and the city behind and report to his unit at Chandigarh. Seema, his eternal support system, hid her tears and cheerfully told him to go answer his call to duty. Her courage seeped through to him, and while he was upset at parting ways from her, he was excited to see what this new phase of his life would spell out for him.

Advay reported earlier than required for his first day of active duty in his unit. His short-cropped hair and cleanly pressed uniform gave him the appearance of a true Army man. His eyes soaked in all the wonderful sights he saw around him; the sun casting its soft glow over the barracks, the Army vehicles and equipment, and various groups of soldiers who were engrossed in many tasks. Excitement coursed through him at the idea of being absorbed into the folds of this thrilling new world.

From the moment he arrived, Advay completely immersed himself in the Army way of life. The routines were strenuous, and the expectations high, especially his stay with the troops where he quickly adapted and rose to the occasion.

Each morning, Advay would wake up at the crack of dawn to the sound of reveille, a bugle call that signaled the start of the day. The crisp morning air was filled with the sounds of soldiers talking and planning for the day ahead. He would then join his comrades on the parade ground for physical training, pushing his limits alongside them in a grueling routine that ultimately strengthened his bond with his fellow soldiers. They encouraged and kept each other going through the toughest of drills, and collectively shared the struggles and triumphs. In the mess hall they would share meals, laughter, and camaraderie. The soldiers exchanged stories and jokes, their spirits lifted and hearts bonded through the threads of togetherness.

After three months of stay with the troops Advay moved to the Officers Mess of his Unit. There he bonded well with his Senior Subaltern and other officers of the Regiment. Advay quickly learned the technical skills required, working under the guidance of experienced officers. The work was demanding, requiring precision and focus, but he thrived in the challenging environment. His fellow officers became like family, each one relying on the knowledge and integrity of others to complete their missions safely and efficiently.

They would gather in small groups during breaks to unwind from the pressure of the work, while sharing experiences with one another and offering advice wherever needed. Advay found himself drawn to the stories of the veterans and their descriptions of the planning and execution of past operations. He absorbed their wisdom, learning not just the practical aspects of his duties, but also the unspoken rules and traditions that defined life in the Army.

The camaraderie within the unit was unlike anything Advay had ever experienced. One of Advay's favorite traditions was the nightly tea sessions. After dinner, the bachelors staying in the Officers Mess would sit in a circle with glasses of hot tea sitting in the center and discuss the day's events. These moments of respite were precious, offering a chance to connect on a personal level. Advay often found himself deep in conversation with his brothers-in-arm, learning about their backgrounds and aspirations, and forging friendships that would last a lifetime.

Through these daily interactions, Advay came to understand the true meaning of brotherhood. It was about trust, loyalty, and mutual respect. It was about knowing that, in times of danger, each man would stand by his side, ready to protect and defend. This sense of unity gave Advay a profound sense of purpose and belonging, fueling his determination to excel, contribute to the success of his unit, and do well for his teammates. Within this close-knit group, Advay discovered his own strengths and limitations. He learned to lean on his comrades for support, and in turn, offered his own strength and encouragement. The bond they shared was a source of immense pride and motivation, driving them all to be better soldiers and better men.

As the weeks turned into months, Advay's skills and confidence grew. He became an integral part of his unit, respected by his peers and superiors alike. The rigorous routines and shared experiences had molded him into a soldier, but more importantly, they had forged relationships that would endure the test of time.

One evening, Advay's Company Commander, Major Srivastava, was preparing to leave for a new assignment. A small farewell gathering was organized at the officer's mess. As the evening wore on, Advay offered to escort Major Srivastava's wife and children back to their quarters.

Suddenly, two men appeared from the shadows, their vile intentions evidently coming forth. They jeered at Mrs. Srivastava, making lewd comments and crass sounds that sent a surge of anger through Advay. He stepped forward to shield the Major's family from the sights of the hooligans, and said in a low but fierce voice, "You will apologize and leave now."

The men laughed, a harsh, jeering sound that echoed in the stillness. One of them sneered, "We won't. Who is here to stop us?"

Advay's response was quick and unforgiving. He lunged at the nearest man, his fists a blur of motion. They were all words and no substance, and Advay could easily take them down. Within moments, both men were on the ground, groaning in pain. Advay stood over them, breathing heavily, his knuckles bruised but his resolve unshaken. "There will always be someone to stop you when you act disrespectfully towards women. Don't think that you can ever get away with something like this. And if I catch you at it once again, my kicks and punches will be much harder," he warned, his voice cold as steel.

News of Advay's actions spread quickly through the unit. He was lauded as a hero, earning the respect of his peers. However, not everyone up the command chain agreed with his heroic acts; he received a summons the next morning from his Commanding Officer (CO), Colonel Bedi. Though Advay knew he had acted in accordance with what the situation had demanded, he was still nervous about the reprimand he was sure to receive from the CO.

As soon as Advay had stepped into his office, the CO curtly said, "Varma, I appreciate your intention to protect the officer's family, but we do not condone violence outside of duty."

Advay shuddered slightly at his hard tone, but he met the CO's gaze unflinchingly and evenly replied, "Sir, they were harassing Mrs. Srivastava. I tried to verbally warn them, but when that did not work, I had to resort to violence."

Colonel Bedi frowned, leaning back in his chair. "I understand why you took those steps. But as soldiers, we must adhere to a code of conduct. Your actions could have serious repercussions, and you need to realize that."

Advay nodded, accepting the scolding, but inside, he knew he had done the right thing. And if such a situation arose again, he would repeat his actions too.

A few weeks later, another incident put Advay's temper against unethical and unjust acts to the test. The incident occurred at the market, where a few jawans, who were shopping for supplies, unexpectedly came under attack by local goons. It began when two army men, Vikram and Rajat, stood their ground against a gang of rowdies mercilessly bullying a shopkeeper. The rowdies, fueled by aggression and arrogance, didn't take kindly to the soldiers' interference. Words escalated into blows, and soon, Vikram and Rajat found themselves outnumbered and battered. Their fellow soldiers, alerted by the commotion, rushed to their aid. The rowdies, sensing trouble, fled the scene. Vikram's face bore the brunt of their fury, nearly costing him his sight.

Advay, his jaw clenched, learned the details. 'These rowdies need a lesson—one they won't forget,' he thundered. Gathering ten men from his unit, he set out to track down the bullies and deliver retribution. The once-bustling market now felt eerily quiet as Advay's team patrolled its narrow alleys, moving like shadows. Information trickled in—a hint here, a whispered rumor there. Finally, they pinpointed the rowdies' likely location—an abandoned warehouse on the outskirts. Advay and his men approached quietly, the element of surprise on their side. Seeing Advay & his men the rowdies blanched, their bravado evaporated.

They barely had time to react before Advay and his men descended upon them. The fight was intense but brief. Advay's training had made his movements precise and devastating, and he landed blows at the speed of lightning. The goons were left battered and bruised by Advay and his men, and a clear message was sent.

Back in the Unit, Advay was summoned once again to Colonel Bedi's office, and this time, the CO looked angrier than ever.

"Beating up people in public? Do you have any idea how badly that could have damaged the perception of people about the Army?" he demanded.

Advay silently said, "With all due respect, Sir, the perception would have been worse if we had not stood up for our men who were beaten up by those goons. If we can't take care of our own, how can we take care of anyone else?"

It was evident that Colonel Bedi was very unhappy about Advay's actions, but Advay's explanation had stumped him. He could not find the words to counter Advay's justification, and grudgingly, he had to drop the issue after giving another stern warning to Advay.

Advay's actions in both these incidents earned him the nickname 'Angry Warrior' within the unit. He became an icon; a soldier who would go to any lengths to protect his comrades and punish wrongdoers. The men admired his courage and resolve, and even the officers couldn't help but respect his dedication.

Life in the Corps of Engineers was never dull. Each day brought new challenges, and new opportunities to prove oneself. Advay embraced every moment, his spirit unbroken, his resolve unwavering. His journey in the Indian Army had only just begun, but the lessons he learned and the bonds he formed in those early days would stay with him forever, shaping him into the soldier and leader he was destined to become.

Chapter 10: The Warrior Owl Soars

Advay had firmly settled into Army life and had proved himself, time and again, to be a dedicated and capable soldier. He seamlessly adapted to the demands and strict routines of his new life, and made worthwhile contributions to various engineering projects that earned him respect from both his peers and superiors. Advay's reputation as a reliable and resourceful officer grew, and he became known for his unwavering commitment to his unit. His leadership skills and fearless nature made him an invaluable asset, and he was often entrusted with challenging assignments.

During one such incident, Advay's brave trait of taking actions that felt right to him even if they went against standardized processes, and the subsequent ire he received from his CO was once again brought to the surface.

He received orders to lead a convoy of twenty-five Army trucks for a deposition of stores at a depot located four hundred kilometers away from their unit. The journey was scheduled to span over two days, with a planned halt midway. Advay, ever the strategist, gathered the drivers and accompanying personnel the day before the mission for a thorough briefing. He had complete faith in the capabilities of his team and thought that the mission could be planned in a more time-efficient way; one that would properly harness the skills of his men and would also get the job done faster.

"We will start the journey at 5:00 am instead of the pre-decided 8:00 am," Advay announced, his voice firm and decisive. The men exchanged surprised glances, but they knew better than to question his judgment. If he had thought of something different for the mission, it would undoubtedly be the better way of executing it. Such was the respect that Advay commanded. "Assemble at 4:30 am with packed meals. No vehicle is to stop unless my lead vehicle halts. If any vehicle goes off-road, it will be left behind, and the driver must reach the destination independently along with the second in command of the convoy who is travelling in the last vehicle," he said and ended his briefing with a crisp nod.

They set off at the crack of dawn. The early morning mist hung low and reduced visibility, which was perhaps why the standard approach was to depart later in the day for the task during winter months, when the sun emerged much later. However, Advay smiled to himself seeing how, like a well-oiled machine, the convoy smoothly moved ahead relying on the powerful headlights that cut through the darkness and illuminated the path ahead. Advay led the convoy with a determined focus, his eyes constantly scanning the road for potential obstacles.

The journey became demanding due to frequent encounters with pothole-ridden roads, unindicated tractors, and cattle crossing the roads. Inclement weather further tested the drivers' focus and attentiveness. However, as Advay had predicted, they rose to the occasion. With only a few brief halts of twenty to thirty minutes when they quickly ate their meals, Advay's belief and enthusiasm rubbed off on them and they were eager to keep going.

By 9:30 pm, they reached their final destination. Advay immediately called Colonel Bedi.

As soon as he reported their safe arrival at the location, the CO's stern voice cracked like a whiplash, saying, "You were supposed to call between 6:00 and 7:00 pm from Destination One! What happened?"

"Sir I am calling from the Final Destination. We pushed through and covered the entire distance in one go, sir," Advay explained calmly.

"And who told you to do that?" he snapped and asked.

"Nobody, sir. As the in-charge of the mission and knowing the capacity of my team, I took a judgment call myself," Advay sincerely replied.

Upon hearing his justification, all hell broke loose and the CO severely reprimanded Advay. Advay patiently held on to the phone, respecting his CO's anger about him not following the rules, but content with the outcome that utilized his team to the full extent and ensured that they were comfortably settled at their Final Destination and would get a good night sleep, and had completed the journey with utmost efficiency, without any untoward complications.

As Advay familarised himself with the tasks they needed to perform there, he was astonished to discover that a two-month timeline had been given for the straightforward task of store deposition, which seemed excessive as per his astute understanding of the work. He scoffed softly and realized that, once again, it was time to switch up the established order of things. The talents and time of his highly capable men would be wasted by spending so much time on this task, and he would not stand for it.

He rounded up the team the next morning and said, "We have a challenge ahead of us. The deposition of these stores is supposed to take two months. But if we work extra hours and finish early, I promise you all something that hasn't been done before."

The men leaned in, curious, and unitedly asked, "What is it, sir?"

"If we complete this in record time, I'll make sure you all go on leave from here. Time to enjoy, see your families, and recharge. But it means pushing ourselves harder than ever. Are you all up for it?" he asked, pumping his fist in the air. His energy, and not to mention the tempting promise he had made of granting them leave, invigorated his men. The team echoed in unison "with you Sir".

Subedar Balwant Singh interjected and said, "Sir, even if we work overtime, the Depot staff has to be there to inspect the stores & stock them in the warehouse".

Advay smiled and calmly responded, "I've already spoken with the Commandant of the Stores Depot, and he assured me that his team will work around the clock if we produce the store for deposition duly rehabilitation."

The next ten days were a blur of relentless work. The team worked in shifts, ensuring that the depot was never silent. The clang of tools as they repaired, and the murmur of voices as they conducted a thorough inspection filled the air day and night. Advay led by example and worked alongside his team; his presence was a constant source of motivation. When the last of the stores were deposited, Advay gathered his exhausted but triumphant team. "You've done an incredible job," he said, pride evident in his voice. "As promised, you're all going on leave. Take this time to rest and be with your loved ones." He signed the leave certificate of twenty-six Jawans, leaving only the drivers & two Jawans to drive the twenty-five Army vehicles back to the Unit.

The men cheered; their fatigue momentarily forgotten in the excitement of the upcoming break. Advay briefed the drivers about the convoy etiquette that had to be strictly followed, and prepared for his solo return journey. Despite the risks and against the laid down instructions, he decided to return at the same speed without co-drivers, pushing the limits once again. When the team returned and reported back to the base, everyone was shocked; deposition of stores had never been done before with such lightning speed. Colonel Bedi couldn't believe it, as this feat was thought of as impossible by everyone.

Without any delay, Colonel Bedi promptly got in touch with the Store Depot's Commandant, who verified that the task had been thoroughly completed. He proceeded to elaborate on how the entire team had performed exceptionally, working round the clock in a highly professional manner under the leadership of young Captain Advay.

Having been mightily impressed by Advay, the Commandant said, "I have never seen an officer of his age exhibit such initiative and 'josh'!"

Colonel Bedi was thrilled to hear such commendation for Advay, and he knew that Advay was a highly worthy addition to the unit. However, although he concealed the pride he felt because Advay had violated established rules and undertaken a risky journey of over four hundred kilometres without any co-drivers.

Scowling at this new incident, he curtly remarked to Advay and the others, "The team completed their task diligently. However, Varma, this doesn't excuse your actions. You can't take matters into your own hands like this every time."

The following day, Advay was served with a counselling letter by the CO for his conduct. The unit praised Advay for achieving an extraordinary feat, but he was saddened to have upset his CO once again. Advay found solace in the fact that he had led his team to do great work. Subsequent to this incident, Advay's popularity within the unit soared. His innovative thinking and undying determination had earned him immense respect. Soldiers admired his ability to think on his feet and execute plans with precision.

His reputation for boldness and ingenuity spread beyond his unit, earning him the nickname 'Warrior Owl' for his ability to improvise, make quick decisions, and achieve remarkable results.

During a brigade-level exercise conducted a few weeks later, the commander tasked the units with finding ways to reduce the construction time of modular bridges by approximately fifteen minutes. The task was daunting, and intense brainstorming sessions ensued. Advay, known for his out of the box thinking, and leveraging the years of intense studies in engineering, examined the traditional methods of bridge construction. He quickly realized that instead of improving the existing construction methodology, a whole new approach was needed.

He proposed constructing the bridge in two parts; initially launching the first half using the traditional method & then rolling down the second part using rollers to complete the bridge. This innovative approach emerged after thoroughly evaluating how it could be executed, the advantages it would bring, and whether it would expose them to any complications.

"We need to think differently," he told his team. "If we can roll the bridge on these rollers, we can save a significant amount of time."

His team looked at him skeptically. "Are you sure about this, sir?" one of his squad members asked him.

Advay nodded confidently. "I am sure. Let's give it a try."

The implementation of Advay's idea produced results that perhaps even he had not expected. When they ran the first drill with his ingenious new method, the construction time had been reduced to such an extent that the officer monitoring it thought he had made a mistake. After rechecking all the facts, he excitedly announced that the new method could optimize their work by a drastic thirty minutes. Like in everything else that he took on, he had tackled this with diligence and thoughtfulness, and it had yielded wonders. As another feather added to his cap, Advay was hailed for securing the best output in a brigade exercise that his unit had seen in a long time.

The Army Commander who visited the exercise area to witness the bridge-level exercise was astounded by the efficiency of Advay's approach and promptly awarded him an on-the-spot commendation card.

After the Army Commander and other senior officers departed, the Brigade Commander patted Advay on the back, saying, "Excellent job, Advay. We are very proud of you." He continued, "I've heard some officers call you the Warrior Owl. For someone as sharp and astute as you've proven to be, I can't think of a more fitting nickname."

The news of Advay's ingenuity soon spread like wildfire. What had started out as a brigade-level exercise had turned into a major transformational exercise in the Army's established processes. Advay had turned around the game, and the benefits of the efficiency that his proposed solution would bring were countless.

Back at his unit, Advay was, once again, summoned by Colonel Bedi. Surprised, since he had not done anything that went remotely against the established rules, he walked into the CO's office. Colonel Bedi stood up to face him and said, "Good work on the bridge construction task. It will help us a lot."

After having received so many reprimands for his actions previously from the CO, it was a welcome change to hear good words for himself. Advay humbly bowed his head in response to the acknowledgment of his hard work. While he was delighted, he was certain the CO had not asked him over to personally praise his work; there had to be something more to this meeting. His suspicions were realized a few moments later when Colonel Bedi said, "You've done good work here, but it's time now for you to make a change."

In response to Advay's questioning gaze, the CO explained, "We need men like you out on the actual field- the battlegrounds. Your logical thinking, willingness to take risks, and most of all, the fierce loyalty you show toward your team will be put to good use there. Your country needs you, and you must answer her call. I am recommending your name for posting to Rashtriya Rifles, in Kashmir."

Advay soon received his posting order and he graciously accepted his new assignment, but several complex thoughts were swirling in his head. This was the chance that he had been waiting for from the very day that he decided to enlist in the army- a chance to fight for his motherland, to fight alongside his brothers, and to fight for defending the liberty of his people. However, the thoughts of his loved ones interspersed the jubilation that he felt at being considered worthy of the posting in Kashmir.

He knew that all of them would be scared about his new assignment. His posting in the regiment in the peace station had relieved them all to a certain extent, for they knew that he would not be facing actual battles or life-threatening situations. Now, however, all that would change. He hated the idea of putting them in such distress, but the calls of his duty were second to none. He braced himself for the difficult conversations he would need to initiate with them.

Jyotika answered the home phone and Advay felt a ripple of happiness course through his body upon hearing her sweet voice. His baby sister was now grown up, and she had transformed into a mature and sensible young woman. She hurriedly called her parents, turned the phone on speaker, and Advay told them about his posting. He heard Sridevi draw in a sharp breath, and Anand's shaky voice as he asked Advay when he was due to leave conveyed just how scared Anand was for the safety and well-being of his son. His parents then fell silent, and Advay's heart raced as he imagined the anguish they must be feeling. Soon, the silence was broken by Jyotika; in a trembling but resolute voice, she said, "I am so proud of you, Bhaiyya. Knowing that you are out there to fight for us will make me feel safer than ever before." Following in their daughter's footsteps of giving Advay the courage to embark on this daunting new journey, Anand and Sridevi wholeheartedly blessed him and assured him that their prayers and good wishes would remain with him wherever he went.

Seema too was initially very disturbed at the idea of him being posted in Kashmir. She normally never lost her composure, but Advay knew she had teared up on the phone as she desperately asked him whether he could refuse the posting, though in her heart she knew that Advay would never be able to live with himself if he passed up this opportunity to serve his country. She took several deep breaths to calm herself, and eventually said, "The forces there will be lucky to have you. I know you will fight your hardest and do your best for the safety of everyone there. Just ensure you stay safe too," she said in a small voice. Unable to bear the profound sorrow in her voice, Advay said, "Don't you worry about me! I am going to be just fine there. And besides, someone has to be there and look for all the nice places we can visit when you come to Kashmir, right?" He heard Seema chuckle on the phone, and it was like music to his ears.

The love and blessings of those closest to him created an impenetrable shield around him; and he boldly ventured to step into the next, challenging phase of his life as an Army officer.

Advay's new reporting base overlooked the pristine, snowclad mountains that Kashmir prided itself upon, and his unit specialized in anti-terrorist operations. The soldiers who were posted there were all seasoned veterans, hardened by the constant threat of attacks and the harsh conditions of the region. The atmosphere was tense but disciplined, and the unit operated with clockwork precision, ready to respond to any threat at a moment's notice.

Upon his arrival, Advay was keenly aware of the challenges ahead. He was supposed to attend the Anti-Terrorist Training School, where he was taught the nuances of tackling terrorist attacks, strategizing and planning defenses, and gathering intel and putting it to good use. He learned with the utmost sincerity for he knew that the teachings of that particular classroom could mean the difference between life and death for him and his people on the battlegrounds.

The Anti-Terrorist Training School was known for its grueling training exercises, designed to push soldiers to their limits. Advay embraced each challenge with open arms, fueled by his wit, courage, and determination. The last stage of the training was a mock exercise simulating a terrorist hostage situation. The scenario adopted real-life conditions, complete with role players acting as terrorists and hostages, and an abandoned building rigged with hidden surprises. Advay dedicated himself wholeheartedly to training and excelled in various test exercises and emerged as a resilient anti-terrorist officer, demonstrating his strength and ability.

After successfully completing his training and excelling in it, he reported to complete the induction formalities with his sub-unit. He had been assigned to serve as the second-in-command of the sub-unit. Advay wasted no time in familiarizing himself with the terrain, the unit's routines, and the men under his command.

Upon reporting to the Operational Room, he was greeted by the company commander, Major Sharma, a stern yet fair officer who had earned the respect of his men through years of service.

"Welcome, Captain Varma," Major Sharma said, extending a hand. "I've heard your performance in the training school's mock exercises has been impressive, but now I look forward to seeing your skills in actual operations. We have a cordon and search operation planned for tomorrow, and I want you to accompany me."

Advay nodded, eager to prove himself. "Yes, sir. I'll be ready."

Major Sharma briefed him on the operation. "We'll move out at night to properly position ourselves and cordon off the village that we need to search. At dawn, we'll commence the search. Your role is crucial. You will be with the Light Machine Gun (LMG) party in the outer cordon. Stay fully alert and await further instructions."

That night, in the perfect disguise offered by the darkness, the sub-unit moved out. The silence was broken only by the soft crunch of boots on dried leaves, and the occasional murmur of commands. Advay felt a mix of excitement and tension as they approached the village. Nothing that he had learned in his training had prepared him for these feelings. This was it, and there was no going back now. Unlike any simulation, every action he took or failed to take here would have implications that were larger than life.

The realization was humbling and daunting at the same time. The moonlight cast eerie shadows on the terrain, but the soldiers moved with practiced stealth. For many of them, it was just another operation. But for Advay, it was the first taste of fighting in field conditions. It was the first time he would be holding the life of his comrades in his hands and had surrendered his life to theirs. His quick thinking and courage would be tested like they had been never before, and it was vital for him to do well in the operation to solidify his place as a worthy addition to the unit.

Advay and the remaining team took their positions in the outer cordon as he had been instructed to do. Major Sharma, before venturing ahead, looked at Advay and encouragingly nodded his head. "Stay sharp. I'll call you ahead when we actually start the search," he remarked and silently but swiftly moved ahead. Advay nodded; his senses heightened. The men around him stayed focused, their eyes scanning the darkness for any signs of movement.

Eventually, the first light of dawn began to creep over the horizon, casting a golden glow over the village. Amidst the silence came the blaring sound of the loudspeaker that had been turned on. The search party announced that the operation was due to begin soon, and urged the villagers to assemble at a pre-decided spot. From his vantage point, Advay saw the villagers troop out of their homes and move towards the gathering spot.

Advay anxiously awaited Major Sharma's signal for him to join the search party, eager to apply his skills from mock exercises to a real operation.

Just then, Havildar Rathi, the LMG commander, spotted two individuals attempting to escape the cordoned area, using a row of thick trees between the inner and outer cordon as cover. Before

Advay could inquire, Rathi suddenly shouted, pointing towards the trees, "Sir, militants!"

Advay's training and instincts took over in an instant. Without a moment's hesitation, he pounced on the light machine gun. The world around him and its vastness ceased to exist; all he could focus on was the barrel of the gun and the figures of the escaping militants. His mind was a blur, but his actions were measured and precise. He could see the militants making a dash for the cover of the trees, their forms silhouetted against the pale light of dawn. The weapon roared to life in his hands, and he used it to cast out a stream of bullets. The noise was deafening, a stark contrast to the silence that he had spent the entire night in. The recoil of the gun slammed against his body, but he held steady, his eyes fixed on the targets. The militants stumbled, falling to the ground under the relentless fire from the LMG.

The entire encounter lasted only a minute, but to Advay, it felt like an eternity.

Before Advay and his team could reach the site where the militants had fallen dead, Major Sharma rushed towards them upon hearing the excessive gunfire. After learning the sequence of events from Havildar Rathi, the company commander appeared visibly upset and reprimanded Rathi, saying, "How did you conclude that these two individuals were militants? They could be civilians trying to avoid the brunt of the cordon and search operations, which is often the case."

He continued, "I understand Captain Advay is new, but you are a seasoned soldier who should understand the implications."

Advay felt a blow to his gut; he realized that he himself should have asked these questions instead of waiting for them to be put forth by the Major. There was a fine line between acting impulsive and acting quickly, and he hoped he had not crossed it.

In the meantime, as Major Sharma was engaged in a tense moment with Advay & Havildar Rathi, Subedar Vijayan and a few soldiers from the inner cordon reached the scene where the individuals lay dead. The individuals, clothed in traditional 'pheran,' looked completely like local civilians. However, upon thorough search, they were found to be militants armed with AK-47s and pistols concealed within their clothing. Perhaps caught off guard by the speed and accuracy of the operation, they had not been able to draw their weapons to retaliate.

Soon after, Major Sharma was informed of the militants' identity and hurried to the site with Advay and his team. Upon realizing what Advay and his team had achieved, Major Sharma was filled with immense joy and embraced Advay, regretting his earlier doubts about them. The soldiers around congratulated Advay and looked at him with profound admiration and respect evident in their eyes.

Word of Advay's fearless and quick response spread quickly through the unit. By the time they returned to base, the story of the young, new officer who had single-handedly taken down two militants was the talk of the camp. Advay's unit commander, Colonel Mehta, was particularly impressed and he asked Advay to meet him at his office later that day.

"Your quick thinking and bravery have set a new standard for this unit," Colonel Mehta said, his voice filled with admiration. "You've earned the respect of your peers and superiors alike."

Advay stood at attention, and his chest swelled up with pride. "Thank you, sir. I just did what I had to do."

Colonel Mehta nodded. "And you did it exceptionally well. We're recommending you for a gallantry award."

Advay's heart skipped a beat. A gallantry award was one of the highest honors a soldier could receive. It was a recognition of bravery and heroism in the face of danger. Advay felt humbled and honored by the news.

The Colonel then continued, "Although you are new & young, you're one of a kind. Seeing your immense potential and skills, I am assigning you as the Company Commander of Echo Company, responsible for one of the most challenging sectors. Are you prepared, Varma?"

"I will always be prepared, Sir, for whatever my nation requires for me," Advay responded firmly and passionately.

The story of the Warrior Owl quickly became a legend; it was told and retold, and with every iteration, the respect that new recruits and seasoned soldiers alike felt for him only grew. In his new position as a Company Commander, he went on to fulfil the destiny written for him in gold, marked by bravery and honor.

Chapter 11: The Metamorphosis of The Owl

Being Company Commander of the Echo Company was both an honor and a challenge, but Advay embraced it with the same determination and bravery that had earned him his previous accolades, and the name of the Warrior Owl resonated loudly from every snow-clad valley in Kashmir.

The area that came under Advay's charge was heavily infested with terrorists and notorious for ambushes on patrol parties and attacks against Army convoys . Knowing the gravity of the situation, Advay started dominating the area with fearless patrolling activities, laying counter-ambushes, raiding hideouts, and making militant movements very difficult. While his operations recovered weapons and ammunition, direct engagement with militants remained elusive.

Recognizing the imminent need for actionable intelligence, Advay began cultivating sources and found two invaluable individuals- 'Kukka Pare', a reformed militant turned informant, and Rashid, a former insider with intimate knowledge of militant activities.

One moonless night, relying on Rashid's information, Advay decided to venture into a marshy, forested area deemed too dangerous for exploration. The terrain was treacherous, unfamiliar, and risky since extraction of his team would be difficult if the operation extended till beyond sunset. Despite these challenges, Advay knew this was an opportunity he couldn't afford to miss.

He gathered his team and briefed them on the mission, emphasizing the risks but also the importance of their objective. He said, "We have information of some of the militants hiding in the dense marshy area & we need to trap them & liquidate'.

"We have to be cautious," he continued, looking at the determined faces of his team. "This area is marshy and difficult to navigate, but this is our chance to neutralise high-value targets. I have faith that we will be victorious in this mission. Do you have faith in me to lead you to that victory?"

His team, ever inspired and in awe of Advay's strong leadership and immense courage, responded with unanimous support.

Guided cautiously by Rashid, the team set out early in the morning. They moved silently, like phantoms, covering each other's steps with precision, their senses alert to every rustle of leaves and even the slightest movement of the wind. The vegetation was thick and made visibility a challenge, and the ground itself was extremely treacherous. However, with Advay's astute planning to back them and he himself leading them from the front, the team easily crossed every obstacle in their path. 'All for One, and One for All' was the essence of the team led by Advay, and true to its spirit, the entire team provided cover to each other as they advanced.

They conducted a comprehensive search of the entire area to locate the militant. Advay led the operation, using precise hand signals to communicate with his team, guiding them flawlessly without uttering a word. By the time they finished their search of a large part of the area, night had fallen and hence Advay decided to settle in the forest area for the remainder of the night. Advay strategically positioned his team on elevated ground, concealed among the cover of trees. The Quick Reaction Team (QRT) formed an outer ring, ready to act swiftly.

At dawn, a soldier stumbled upon a concealed chamber camouflaged by foliage. The chamber led to a meticulously designed tunnel—a clandestine artery pulsing with menace. Advay was surprised at this unexpected revelation. He and his team carefully descended into it and explored the tunnel. Advay nodded grimly as he took in the sight that met their eyes upon their descent; it was a sophisticated hideout, complete with a radio station, rations, and an arsenal of 62 small and high-caliber weapons. It was clear they had found the hideout of the top militant commander.

With a catch of large stockpiles of weapons and ammunition, Advay has broken the militants' backbone, forcing them into scattered retreats. On returning to the base, he immediately reported the discovery to his Commanding Officer who arrived with the Brigade Commander and a group of journalists. The operation, although did not result in the militant's capture, was a significant success for the anti-terrorist efforts due to the substantial number of arms and ammunition seized by his unit, and hence made headlines. Advay, being the mastermind behind the well-planned and executed mission, was once again in the news for his exceptional bravery and leadership.

Advay's strategic use of intel and fearless action cemented his sub-unit's reputation for efficiency and bravery, and tales of their courage echoed in the valley. To add to his expanding list of well-deserved and hard-earned victories, Advay's valour was recognized in the form of his being awarded the Sena Medal for his gallant act of eliminating two militants in his maiden fighting operation.

When he shared the news of his newest accolade with his family and Seema, their pride and joy were clearly discernible despite the distance separating them. As their conversations grew less frequent, he cherished each moment spent speaking with them.

There were moments when his eyes became numb and his heart ached, but he quickly shook off the feeling by reminding himself that he was a part of the elite few who got a chance to serve for their country. He felt blessed to have a family that understood and wholeheartedly supported his duty, making the prolonged separation more bearable.

Though Advay had destroyed the militants' operating base, he was yearning to cause more damage and completely cripple their activities. He made up his mind to go after the top military commander operating in the area. He wanted to track down and eliminate the most dreaded self-styled divisional commander, Hamid Gada. The busting of the main hideout had made Gada vulnerable, and Advay wanted to prey on this vulnerability.

Advay correctly surmised that Gada had likely begun seeking refuge in safe houses scattered throughout the village, frequently changing his whereabouts. Advay put his network of informants on Gada's trail and told them to follow him aggressively. Shortly later, he started getting reports of Gada's movement regularly, however every time luck favoured the militant and he managed to slip out of every location by the time Advay & his team cordoned the area. Hamid Gada was a master magician in the game of disguise and melted like a chameleon in the crowd since no security forces had not seen him till now.

Advay refused to settle for minor victories. With his ultimate goal in clear view, he became obsessed with capturing the notorious militant, Hamid Gada. He ramped up his efforts, meticulously gathering information from all available sources. Despite their newfound direction, they remained no closer to locating Gada. Frustration simmered, yet Advay maintained his calm, stoic demeanor for the sake of his team.

A few days later, their patience was rewarded. One of Advay's team members, Havildar Chauhan came running in with a scrap of paper in his hand and excitedly said, "Sir, you were right about Mama! He really has come through for us."

Mama was a young, local boy who had once come under the radar of the Army for creating a nuisance and working as a pickpocket in the area. When they had once got their hands on him, the others had dismissed him as a good-for-nothing, but Advay's keen and wise eyes had seen something in him. He believed Mama could be highly resourceful and valuable if his mind was put to good use. Advay met him after that in secret, mentored him to change his ways, and trained him to become an informant. The team had their reservations about this, but Advay trusted his own instincts.

Havildar Chauhan held a note scribbled by Mama, asking Advay to meet him later that night for some crucial information. Without expressly hearing it from him, Advay knew it would be about Hamid Gada; he could feel it in his very bones. He arranged a clandestine meeting with Mama at roughly eight in the night and was shocked to hear that Gada was allegedly operating from an isolated house within their area of operation. While he trusted his source, he did not want to lead his team to another dead end.

"Is this confirmed news?" he sharply asked Mama.

The boy, who looked much more mature and confident since he had turned his life around with Advay's help, nodded solemnly and said, "It is 100% confirmed news."

Advay nodded his thanks and hastily returned to base; he had a mission to complete now. He quickly briefed his team on the new developments and despite the late hour, he saw a fire of enthusiasm raging in them to set out to capture the dreaded militant. Without wasting a moment, the team geared up, assembled, and moved quickly to the location. The house, which looked thoroughly deserted, was searched from top to bottom, but no one was found.

Many team members believed that their target had again slipped away, but Advay's gut feelings strongly told him to remain there and search more. He remembered the look of absolute dedication on Mama's face, and believed that there was a lot of merit to the intel.

While the team was starting to leave, which was the usual practice they followed to exit places of their search operations, Advay held up a decisive hand and indicated for them to stop and stay still. He silently lay down on the ground, pressing his ears against the floor to listen for any sounds coming from the building's footing. Soon he realised that there was some movement beneath; it confirmed his suspicions that there was a hideout in the building's basement. With a sweeping motion of his wrist, he told them to search the entire house again.

During the second search, one of the team members noticed something unusual about a large cupboard embedded in the wall and the planks of the cupboard could be removed. Advay, who was immediately called there, tugged on one of the planks and discovered that it easily came apart. He quickly told his team to remove them all, and it led them to discover an opening leading to a basement hideout. As soon as they uncovered the entrance, they came under heavy fire from the militants inside. The firing from multiple weapons told Advay that there were approximately two to three militants. Advay quickly moved his team outside to regroup and plan their next move. He knew they needed to act fast to prevent the militants from escaping under the cover of darkness. Within no time they established a ring of cordon around the house with troops taking up positions on likely escape routes.

Advay, realising that they needed to quickly act, gathered and told his team, "We need to expose the hideout from outside, and the only way to do that is to place explosives and blow it through to make an opening." Advay apprised them that it was highly risky and the hideout was likely to have vents through which the militants were firing on the Army team. "I will crawl from one side & place the explosive near the likely hideout, the QRT should provide me cover and the LMG team deployed as 'Stops' should guard the escape routes," he told his men.

The team exchanged uncertain glances, for it was a very dangerous move. They hesitantly tried to voice their concerns and a few of them volunteered to place the explosive. Advay, however, waved a dismissive hand and said, "I'm your commander. I will lead, facing any challenge that comes first."

Even in that tense moment, Advay's integrity and passion as a leader came forth and the admiration his men felt for him grew multifold.

And hence, without concern for his personal safety, Advay led the operation from the front. He crawled towards the basement area amidst a hail of bullets, carrying explosives to breach the hideout. With precision and calmness, he set up the explosives and hastily retreated to a safe distance. The blast was powerful, collapsing the basement wall and exposing the militants. The team immediately opened fire, neutralizing the threats within moments.

The militants were identified as Hamid Gada, Mohammed Darr, and Amir Sheikh, each carrying a bounty of five lakhs on their heads.

The operation, in one single blow, had eliminated three major militants who were enemies of peace. It was a significant victory made even more special by the fact that it had been so efficiently yet perfectly planned and had involved a lot of quick thinking and improvisation. Not many people could have led a team of men in such a dynamic operation, successfully eliminated the targets, and ensured that there were no casualties. That's what made Advay such an exceptional leader.

Advay's name was recommended for the Shaurya Chakra, one of the highest military honors for bravery. Months later, as the prestigious award was bestowed upon him, the feeling was surreal for Advay. What was an even better feeling for him, however, was the fact that Havildar Chauhan and another member of his team also received the Sena Medal for their courage in the operation. While his personal victory made him very happy, he was happier about the fact that he had helped his men win their well-deserved accolades too.

The Warrior Owl thus continued to soar, leading with courage, honor, and an unyielding dedication to duty.

After doing brilliantly in the Rashtriya Rifles, Advay earned great respect for his tactical thinking and bravery. His success in multiple operations made him one of the best leaders that the unit had ever seen. As his time in Kashmir came to an end, he prepared to return to his parent unit, the Engineer Regiment.

Before leaving, Advay gathered his team for a final briefing. "You made an incredible team," he said, looking at his men with pride. "It has been an honor serving alongside you all. Each of you has taught me a lesson or two on unity and courage that I will never forget."

A chorus of sounds could be heard after Advay's last briefing. Cries of, "You were the best leader we could have asked for!" and "Sir, we'll miss you!" could be discerned amidst the general noise. "Sir, stories of your bravery and exploits will always have a special place within our battalion's history, the only officer to have been awarded Sena Medal & Shaurya Chakra," remarked Havildar Rathi, his eyes ablaze with admiration.

And thus, with heartfelt farewells, Advay departed for his new unit. His experiences in Kashmir had not only honed his skills but also strengthened his resolve. Returning to his parent unit, he brought with him a wealth of knowledge and a renewed commitment to serve, ready to tackle new challenges alongside his old comrades.

The atmosphere in his unit was very different as compared to the intense, high-stakes environment in Kashmir. Instead of constant patrols and firefights, the focus was back on combat engineering &

technical operations. Young officers of the unit were excited to have him back and eager to hear his stories. One evening, they all gathered in the mess hall, catching up over cups of steaming tea.

"How was the experience there, Sir? We heard you were made the Company Commander of a unit!" remarked Captain Kamlesh.

"It was...something else," Advay replied with a small smile, leaning back in his chair. "The terrain, the weather, and always being on alert; it was one challenge after another that really kept us sharp. But the team's spirit was what really made the difference. I was lucky to have some good men working with me."

Another subaltern, listening to Advay's stories with his eyes widened with interest, asked, "Sir, you have done multiple operations, with two gallantry awards. Which one was the most thrilling or difficult operation you led?"

Advay grinned and said, "Every day felt like an operation!" His light-hearted humor set a very relaxed mood for the entire group, and upon their subsequent insistence, he eventually told them about his legendary victory over the top militant commanders.

Early next morning, Advay stood at attention as he awaited his new commanding officer, Colonel Menon. In the time that he had been away, a lot had changed at the Unit, as was the usual practice. And that included a change in leadership, and Advay was eager to meet his CO.

"At ease, Varma," Colonel Menon said as he entered the room, and extended his hand toward Advay. "I've heard a lot about you from

Colonel Bedi. He speaks very highly of your bravery and leadership. And I know he is not one to give away praises that easily!"

His new CO's pleasant demeanour and memories of the various, colorful encounters he had had with Colonel Bedi brought a slight smile to Advay's face.

"Thank you, Sir. I've always aimed to serve to the best of my abilities," he replied, shaking the Colonel's hand firmly.

Colonel Menon nodded, a gleam of respect alight in his eyes. "I expect great things from you. It will be a pleasure working with you."

"Yes, Sir. I won't let you down," Advay assured him, feeling a strong bond of respect forming between them.

In the days that followed, Advay quickly settled back into his role, bringing with him the combat experience and strategic knowledge gained from his posting in Kashmir. His transition back to the technical environment was seamless, and he soon began to make significant contributions to his unit's tasks. His leadership skills, sharpened in the intense conditions of active conflict, proved invaluable as he managed teams, oversaw complex engineering tasks, and implemented innovative solutions to logistical challenges. His presence boosted morale and inspired a renewed sense of purpose among his peers.

Late one evening, Advay got a summons from Colonel Menon. He had come to thoroughly enjoy his interactions with the CO, who was a highly decorated officer along with being well read and exceptionally intelligent. Advay always felt like he could learn a lot from him.

"Varma, you've done exceptional work here and in Kashmir," Colonel Menon began, looking at him with a glint in his eyes that gave Advay a hint about the challenge that was going to come his way. "Have you ever considered taking the Defense Services Staff College (DSSC) exam?"

Advay raised an eyebrow, surprised. "The DSSC exam? I don't know too much about it, but I have heard that it's extremely competitive."

"It is," the Colonel confirmed, nodding solemnly. "About 1,800 to 2,000 candidates appear each year, and only the top 250 are selected. It's one of the most prestigious courses training officers for higher ranks and appointments. I feel you have the potential to be among the best of the best, and frankly, the Army could do with a person like you in a higher-up position."

Advay leaned forward, intrigued, and said, "I am honored that you think me capable enough for this, Sir. I will surely look into it and give it my best!

"The Staff College's crest is an owl perched on swords," Colonel Menon continued, a smile playing on his lips. "They call the students 'Wise Owls.' And for you, the Warrior Owl, it seems like the most fitting next step."

Advay took a deep breath and smiled; it almost seemed like a cosmic connection had been formed. Right from his very birth when he had been christened with the name by the hospital staff to the

VERSES KINDLER PUBLICATION

present times when he had become renowned in the Army with the same, it seemed like he always had a close bond with those magnificent birds of the night.

After his CO had revealed the surprising symbology of the DSSC, Advay too believed that fate had worked its magic once again to place him on the path it had chosen for him.

Colonel Menon leaned back in his chair, looking serious. "You have the skills and the experience. More importantly, you have the right mindset. I'll help you in any way I can."

Advay left the meeting with a renewed sense of purpose. Preparing for the DSSC exam would be demanding, but he was ready for the challenge. He immersed himself in his studies, balancing his regular duties with rigorous exam preparation. The exam covered a wide range of topics, and even the slightest error could prove to be his undoing since he would be competing with the smartest minds from all over. Advay's background in both engineering and frontline combat gave him a unique perspective that proved beneficial in his preparation.

On the day of the exam, Advay felt a mix of nerves and determination. The competition was intense, with many of the best people from the Armed forces vying for a limited number of spots. He focused only on the task at hand, recalling the discipline and focus that had served him well in the field. The exam was challenging, testing not only his knowledge but also his analytical and problem-solving skills.

Advay tackled each paper methodically, drawing on his diverse experiences to inform his answers. When it was over, he felt a sense of relief but also uncertainty. He knew he had done his best, but the results were out of his hands.

Months later, the results were announced. Advay had made it into the top 250, securing his place at the prestigious DSSC. The news was met with cheers from his unit, who were proud of their comrade's achievement.

Colonel Menon congratulated him warmly. "I knew you could do it. You're going to do great things at DSSC."

Advay's time at the DSSC was intense and enriching. The 10-month course was designed to prepare officers for higher command and staff appointments. The rigorous training was both professionally and intellectually demanding, but Advay thrived in the challenging environment.

The DSSC experience broadened his perspective, exposing him to new ideas and strategies that would be crucial in his future roles. He formed bonds with fellow officers from the Navy, Air Force, and also different branches of the military, learning from their experiences and sharing his own. The atmosphere of mutual respect and camaraderie reminded him of his time in Kashmir, but with a new layer of academic intensity and strategic depth.

As the Staff course was coming to an end, the atmosphere suddenly grew increasingly uneasy. Whispers of unrest along the borders began to circulate among the officers. There were no concrete details, just a palpable sense of tension that had filled the air.

Advay could feel the weight of something brewing, an undefined threat that made him very restless. After every discussion with his comrades, each of whom was as eager as he was to know what was going on, the unease only grew. Advay's mind kept drifting back to his unit, the men he led, and the responsibilities he had left behind.

His desperation to return to his unit and understand the unfolding situation intensified daily. The sense of duty and the need to be with his comrades in uncertain times drove him to hasten his preparations for departure. Advay knew that his place was with his unit, ready to face whatever challenges lay ahead together, like an unbreakable and unstoppable force.

Chapter 12: Heeding The Country's Call

As soon as Advay stepped foot on his base, it was very evident that something was amiss in the atmosphere. The usual camaraderie among the soldiers was replaced by an extremely tense, unnerving atmosphere charged with a different kind of energy. Soldiers rushed about with a sense of urgency, their expressions grim and focused. Conversations were hushed, and the weight of some impending calamity hung heavy in the air.

Though Advay did not know the details, he could feel it in his very bones that his motherland had called upon her sons and daughters in the forces to come to her aid.

The unit had a deserted look & he learned that the unit had moved out of their base, leaving only one company behind in the rear.

He hurriedly approached the Officer-in-Charge of the rear party, Major Arya and explained that he had just returned to the base after ten months. Major Arya, who was junior to Advay, knew about his posting and welcomed Advay to the folds of the unit. Arya gave him a brief about the situation that had unfolded; he gritted his teeth and angrily remarked, "Sir,Pakistani militants and troops have invaded areas under our administration along the line of control. They attacked like the true weaklings that they are. We are fighting back. A war is set to happen in Kargil."

Major Arya also informed Advay that their unit had already been deployed on the frontlines to handle some sensitive operations.

Advay's anger surged, causing him to tremble with rage, eager to join the unit as soon as possible.

Cutting Advay, Arya informed him that the assignments made by his CO required him to stay in the rear and coordinate the movement of important equipment and stores to the war front. He dutifully but reluctantly took on the role. Despite being well aware of the critical nature of his assigned role, Advay felt a burning desire to join his unit in the field.

He managed his responsibility with precision and efficiency, ensuring that every piece of equipment reached its destination on time. His organizational skills and attention to detail were impeccable, and his efforts played a critical role in supporting the front-line troops.

However, he longed to be in the thick of battle. Each convoy he dispatched felt like a reminder of the action he was missing. Every urgent report and status update that came from the front lines only heightened his unease. It eventually got to a point that became unbearable to Advay; the thought of staying behind while his unit faced the enemy felt like agony. He wanted to be out there to serve with his unit, directly combating the enemy and taking out as many as he could in the process.

He made up his mind to go to the front lines, sharing the risks and challenges with his comrades. He could not wait any longer.

While he was consumed by a determination to reach the operational area as soon as possible, he realized that a high-stakes responsibility had been placed on his shoulders which he could not shirk off. He rushed to discuss if Major Arya would be able to handle the critical tasks in the rear.

Advay recognized Major Arya as a dynamic and highly capable member of his unit, confident in his ability to manage the tasks. Advay promptly briefed him about the situation. Understanding Advay's perspective, Major Arya assured him of his complete dedication to assuming the responsibilities. However, Major Arya raised a concern and enquired, "Sir, Colonel Menon is already far ahead on the frontline. How will you seek his permission to leave for Leh?".

Advay had already foreseen this problem. However, time was of the essence, and Advay knew he had to act quickly. He nodded solemnly at Major Arya and said, "I've got it covered." And without wasting another moment, he raced ahead to take a bold step.

He rushed to the Brigade Commander's office, his resolve unshakable. It was unprecedented for any officer to go above the orders issued by their CO and directly approach the Brigade Commander, but Advay told himself that these were unprecedented times too which required drastic and quick measures. The Brigade Commander was absorbed in reviewing maps and coordinating strategies when he was interrupted by a confident knock on the door. When he looked at Advay, without even waiting to be asked to come into the office, Advay firmly stated, "Sir, I have not been able to speak to my CO as he is not reachable, and I need to be at the war front with my men."

He stood in rapt attention while the Brigade Commander considered his request. Before he could raise any objections, Advay

188

quickly said, "I have briefed Major Arya about coordinating logistics from the rear and I have full faith in his abilities. I can coordinate logistics from the field and support my men directly. My place is with my unit and I need to be there."

The Brigade Commander was swayed by Advay's sincerity of wanting to be with his unit and his resourcefulness at ensuring that his absence at the rear end would not compromise any operations. He really could think of no reason not to honor Advay's request. If anything, Advay was an asset & his presence in the operational area would only add to the crisis management abilities of the CO.

After a tense silence, Brigadier Singh nodded. "Very well, Advay. You have my consent. I will try to speak to your CO in this regard but, you may have to manage the logistics on your own."

"Will do, Sir," Advay replied and saluted the Brigade Commander. Relieved at being given the chance to fight alongside his men, he directed all his efforts toward reaching the battleground as fast as possible.

Advay immediately coordinated with the Air Force, leveraging a close connection from his College DSSC days. His fellow course mate,Wing Commander Nair, was more than willing to assist.

"Sir, my unit is out there fighting in Leh. I need to be with them. Can you help me?" Advay emphatically asked over the phone.

"Consider it done. One IL-76 is leaving for Leh tomorrow morning with logistics & troops," Nair replied, sensing Advay's urgency to join his comrades in the face of danger, and wanting to help this exceptionally brave officer in any way that he could.

True to his word, Nair made the necessary arrangements and Advay boarded the IL-76 early next morning, the aircraft's engines roaring to life as it took off towards Leh. The flight was tense, the soldiers on board sharing a common unspoken understanding of the dangers ahead. As the aircraft soared over the rugged terrain, Advay's mind was focused on the mission ahead; but in the deafening silence of the ride, thoughts about his loved ones encroached on his mind. He pictured his parents' comforting faces, Seema's dazzling smile, and Jyotika's merry laughter; they each became symbols of strength and power for him. The uncertainty of war loomed large, but their unwavering support fueled his resolve. He silently vowed to return to them, no matter the outcome.

Upon landing in Leh, Advay wasted no time and found out about the location of his unit from the 'Report Centre'. He identified an Army truck heading towards his unit's location and hitched a ride with it. The journey was long and arduous, the roads winding through the harsh mountainous landscape. But Advay's mind was numb to everything around him. He had a clear target in sight- bring down the enemies and help his comrades, and anything besides this target held no importance for him at the moment.

By the time he reached his destination, the sun was beginning to set. The unit was in the thick of preparations when Advay unexpectedly arrived there. The entire unit was delighted; his presence had always been like a stabilizing anchor that helped them tide through uncertain times and difficulties; and such a stabilizing force was important for them now more than ever. He was their leader, and having him there made every challenge seem more manageable. However, they had to keep their joy under wraps because from the thundering tone in which Colonel Menon said, "Varma, you are not supposed to be here," it was evident that the CO was furious about this turn of events.

The Colonel's immense anger initially surprised Advay, as the usually calm and composed leader rarely lost his temper. Advay had always shared a good relationship with him, which made the reprimand sting even more. Despite the shock, Advay quickly accepted the CO's fury, understanding that he had indeed disobeyed orders by leaving the base to reach Leh.

"How could you go against my clear orders? You were supposed to coordinate logistics from the rear!" Colonel Menon's voice boomed.

"Sir, I couldn't stay behind while my men are out here. I need to be with them," Advay pleaded. "I got permission from the Brigade Commander, and I briefed Major Arya on what needed to be done at the rear end," Advay said, feeling the wrath of his CO but unshakeable in his resolve of having done the right thing.

Colonel Menon's eyes narrowed. "I don't care whose permission you have taken and what arrangements you have made. You will go back immediately and do the task I assigned you."

"Please allow me to stay, Sir. You know I can contribute a lot here. My place is with you and the troops on the field" Advay insisted, his determination absolute.

After a long, tense pause, Colonel Menon sighed. Advay's statement about the amount he could contribute on the field had left the Colonel without any counter. He knew Advay was one of his best men, and since the rear end operations had been handled, Advay truly could work wonders for their field operations. "Fine, you can stay. But one misstep, or one more contradiction of my authority, and you're back to base. Understood?"

"Yes, Sir, loud and clear. Thank you," Advay sincerely replied, relief washing all over him.

After gaining the CO's rather reluctant approval, Advay threw himself into the unit's operations. He caught up on everything that he had missed, learned the wonderful work they had pulled off in a short span of time, and gathered his thoughts about the numerous tasks still ahead of them.

It was only once he had reached the heart of the operations that he realized how high the stakes were. Even a single mistake could cost them heavily, and the pride and honor of the entire country rested upon their shoulders. While this momentous realization was enough to make many people afraid and uncertain about what was to come, it had the opposite effect on Advay. He felt more courageous than ever; it was like a fierce beast had awoken in him. That beast knew no fear or hesitation; it simply knew bravery.

The situation at the front was incredibly tense. The ceaseless barrage of gunfire from the enemy formed a lethal cadence, resonating throughout the terrain. Army convoys could only move during brief halts in the firing, and they rushed to transport essential supplies and personnel in such periods.

Subedar Patel, a member of Advay's unit, was tasked to ensure the smooth movement of trucks with critical supplies during the period of non-firing. During one such move, as the convoy made its way through the exposed terrain, the silence was shattered by the sudden resumption of enemy fire. Bullets and shrapnel tore through the air, striking the truck with lethal precision.

Subedar Patel, the driver, and another jawan in the truck all groaned in pain as shrapnel embedded itself deeply in their bodies and the splinters tore away at their skin.

Back at the base, Advay received the urgent distress call. "This is Unit Ten from near Destination Six. We have injured personnel." The voice was shaky, and Advay could sense the fear and urgency.

"This is Unit One, we're coming to get you!" Advay shouted into the radio.

Turning to his CO, he hastily explained the situation. "Sir, I need to get them out. They're pinned down and injured."

Colonel Menon, though still angry about Advay's previous disobedience, knew that he was one of the few men capable enough to rescue the fallen soldiers. He quickly nodded and said, "Go, Varma and bring them back safely."

Advay grabbed his gear and jumped into a vehicle. The sounds of gunfire seemed even louder as he sped towards the trapped truck, every bump in the road a reminder of the danger. As he approached, he saw the damaged vehicle and his injured comrades huddled behind it, trying to stay out of the line of fire.

He skidded to a halt and jumped out, bullets flying past him. He crouched low and moved towards his comrades. The driver was slumped over, blood trickling down his face, while Subedar Patel clutched his leg, grimacing in pain.

"We need to move, now!" Advay urgently said, lifting the injured driver onto his shoulders.

He quickly helped all the wounded into the back of his vehicle. As he did, the firing intensified, making the air thick with dust and noise. Advay shielded his comrades as best as he could, his own safety a secondary concern.

"Hold on, we're getting out of here!" he shouted over the cacophony to reassure them.

With the injured men secured, Advay jumped back into the driver's seat and floored the gas pedal. The vehicle roared to life and sped back towards their base, dodging potholes and debris. The journey back felt like an eternity, but Advay's focus never wavered. His only thoughts were on getting his men to safety.

Finally, they burst through the gates of the Military Hospital complex. Medics were already rushing towards them as Advay stopped the vehicle. He felt a wave of exhaustion and relief wash over him with the knowledge that his comrades were in safe hands. His bravery and quick-thinking had been instrumental in saving his comrades' lives.

Advay keenly immersed himself in every task where he believed he could contribute, be it back-end strategizing or front-end combatting. . It was during one such preparation that he learned about one of the operations that needed to be carried out on priority so as to minimize the risks of casualty to the assaulting team- the mine clearances. Their intel revealed that the enemy had placed strategic land mines on a few crucial locations, and a team was to be dispatched within two days.

When an opportunity arose to volunteer as the team leader of this mine clearance team, Advay knew this was the kind of task for which he had been drawn to the battleground. Quickly assessing the demands of the task and after being satisfied that he would be suitable for it, he went to the CO and declared, "Sir, I'll lead the team."

Colonel Menon, who had softened toward Advay upon seeing the immense value that he brought to their operations, nodded softly. Truth be told, the team needed someone exactly like Advay. His strategic thinking, ability to lead from the front, and extensive training would be their biggest asset. Impressed with the initiative Advay had shown, the CO gave him clearance to lead the task.

The wise warrior owl was ready to soar its wings.

Two days later, Advay and his team were airlifted to the base of the first peak, which was supposed to be the most heavily mined by the enemy. The cold air bit at their skin as they prepared to undertake the dangerous task. Advay could clearly discern the nervousness on his men's faces, but it was mingled with a fierce resolve. They were each committed to doing what was needed of them, no matter the risks.

"Stay sharp, everyone. We will move slowly and carefully," Advay instructed as they disembarked from the aircraft.

The process of mine clearance under fire from the enemy was incredibly difficult and nerve-wracking. One wrong move could plunge them all into the clutches of death, but Advay had vowed to prevent that from happening under his watch. He had extensively briefed his team on how to go about the operation, the safety measures they needed to follow, and the utmost vigilance they needed to display.

Under his impeccable leadership, Advay and his team moved methodically, under the cover of darkness, using mine detectors and probes to find and disarm the hidden explosives.

"We're doing good work. We just have to keep going," Advay murmured, watching as one of his youngest soldiers, Lance Naik Yadav, carefully and expertly disarmed a mine.

By midnight, they had cleared the first peak and by dawn, the assaulting infantry captured the location. The sense of accomplishment equaled the tension brought by the knowledge that two more such peaks awaited them. They pressed on, and by the second night, they had successfully cleared the second peak. This was also occupied by its own infantry column after a fierce battle. Advay's team camped at the base of the third peak, exhausted but determined, and jubilant at the important work they had successfully completed.

"Thank you for trusting me as your leader, I am so proud of what we have accomplished together. We just have one more location to complete," Advay encouragingly told his team.

'Sir, with you guiding us, we truly believe we can achieve anything!" said Subedar Kishan, and the entire team enthusiastically agreed.

The following day, they tackled the third peak with the same methodical precision. By the end of the third day, they had cleared all three peaks that had been assigned to them and the first objective was under the control of the Indian Army. Following this, another column comprising infantry and engineers was assigned the task of capturing the final objective.

Another engineering team tasked with clearing the minefield at the final destination had not arrived due to heavy enemy fire along their route. Understanding the critical importance of this task, Advay decided to volunteer to proceed ahead and ensure its timely execution. His precise planning and instructions to his team had led them to finish the clearance of the first three locations before time. Since they were already close to the final destination and had flawlessly implemented the same kind of work, Advay felt it was their duty to see the mission through to the end.

He immediately connected with the Sector Commander and communicated his readiness to take on the next task. Without a second's delay, he continued and asked, "Permission to proceed to the final objective, Sir."

"Clearing mines of the first three peaks was itself a big task for your team. They may be exhausted. Let the other assigned team do the last one," the Sector Commander replied, concerned.

"We're already here, Sir. We can finish the job," Advay insisted.

After a moment's consideration, the Sector Commander nodded. "Alright, I'm giving you the go-ahead. Be careful and stay safe."

The team quickly made their way to the final destination and moved cautiously, each step taken with utmost care. The air was thick with tension as they navigated the treacherous terrain. Advay's eyes keenly scanned the ground, searching for any signs of the deadly devices hidden beneath.

"Keep your eyes open and stay focused," Advay instructed his team. "We're almost there. We just have to get through this final challenge."

The soldiers nodded, their faces set with determination. They trusted Advay implicitly, knowing that his leadership had guided them safely through numerous challenging situations before, and it would do so again. The team leader of the assaulting infantry column was highly impressed with Advay's sense of commitment and his josh to accomplish the task.

As they reached the base of the final peak, Advay gathered his team for a final briefing. The mountain loomed above them, a formidable challenge waiting to be won.

"This is it, everyone," Advay said, his voice steady. "We need to clear this final peak to secure the complete area. Move slowly, work methodically, and watch each other's movement. We've got this."

The team split into pairs, each soldier moving with extreme caution. The sound of their careful footsteps and the occasional beep of the mine detectors were the only noises breaking the silence. Hours passed as they painstakingly cleared a path up the mountain. By midnight, they had almost completed their task. The sense of accomplishment was palpable, but so was the accompanying tension of the dangerous task they were engaged in.

As they neared the summit, Advay stepped forward, his mine detector sweeping the ground in front of him. Suddenly, there was a sharp click. Before he could react, a deafening explosion shook the air from a deceitfully placed and well-camouflaged landmine. A burning pain seared through his right foot, and he was thrown to the ground.

Two more of his soldiers, Lance Naik Yadav and Naib Subedar Chauhan, were also hit by splinters from the blast, their cries of pain mingling with the chaos.

This was followed by an intense firefight from both sides. The determined Indian forces relentlessly pounded the enemy's position, swiftly capturing the most critical location.

Despite being seriously injured, Advay remained concerned for the safety of his team, ensuring they stayed sheltered within the folds of the gigantic mountain base, while the injured soldiers received medical attention from the accompanying personnel as they awaited the rescue team.

Within a short while, the sound of rotor blades filled the air. The helicopter hovered above, lowering a stretcher for the injured. However, there was a problem—due to weight restrictions and the approaching darkness, the helicopter could only take two people.

"Sir, you're the most severely injured. You need to go," Subedar Kishan and Havildar Pawar insisted and had almost started hoisting Advay toward the stretcher. Few other soldiers too were eagerly nodding at the suggestion of Advay first being taken to safety, since he had borne the most direct and disastrous impact of the blast.

"No," Advay said firmly, refusing the help from the soldiers. "Take them first," he insisted.

"But, Sir—" someone tried to reason with Advay when they were sharply cut off.

"That's an order. Get going with it," Advay vehemently said, his eyes blazing with determination.

With no time to argue and no way that they could persuade Advay to leave, the other soldiers lifted the two injured jawans onto the helicopter. As it took off, Advay watched it disappear into the dimming sky, happy that he had fulfilled his ultimate duty as a team leader and ensured the safety of his men.

The infantry commander had arrived at the site and commended Advay and his team for their exceptional efforts in capturing the final objective against overwhelming odds. Meanwhile, Advay's condition continued to worsen, his pain becoming intolerable. Recognizing the urgency, the commander swiftly arranged for a doctor from his team to attend to Advay. Knowing the slim chances of a helicopter returning soon, they began preparing to evacuate Advay on a stretcher. Despite the uncertainty, a few members of Advay's team held onto hope, inspired by Advay's unwavering resolve.

And just when it seemed all hope was lost, the faint sound of rotor blades echoed through the night. The helicopter, miraculously, was returning. As a stretcher extended and his men hurriedly got Advay onto it, he immediately asked the pilot, "It is so dark! How did you return at this time for a rescue operation?"

"I was honored to take a risk for an officer like you, Sir," came the immediate reply. "Seeing what you did for your men, the kind of bravery you exhibited, inspired me immensely." Advay, through the colossal pain that had taken over his body but refused to affect his spirit, managed a slight smile.

The journey back to Leh Hospital was tense. Advay's injuries were severe, and time was of the essence. And unfortunately, a lot of it has been lost already.

Upon arrival, the doctors quickly assessed the situation. The damage to Advay's foot was extensive, and amputation was the only option.

When Advay awoke after the painful surgery he had had to endure, the reality of his situation hit him hard. His right foot was gone, replaced by a bandaged stump. The pain was intense, but even more so was the emotional weight of what he had lost.

"How are you feeling?" Colonel Menon asked, standing by his bedside.

"I'm alive and well, Sir," Advay replied, his voice steady despite the turmoil inside.

"You're much more than that, Varma. You're a hero. Your actions saved lives. I speak on behalf of the entire Army when I say that we are proud to have an officer like you," Colonel Menon said, the admiration evident in his voice.

In the aftermath of the surgery, Advay faced many struggles, the least of which was the excruciating pangs of physical pain. He had difficulty mentally coming to terms with what had happened, and how much his life would change. No part of him regretted what he had done; the news of Naib Subedar Chauhan and Lance Naik

Yadav's smooth recovery took his mind off his own challenges and made him genuinely happy.

A few days later, he received news that he was to be awarded the Veer Chakra. Being one of the most prestigious recognitions of one's valor and courage, it would engrave Advay's name forever in the pages of Army history where the tales of his exemplary bravery would remain captured till the end of time, ready to keep inspiring others.

As soon as his health had stabilized and he was fit enough for travel, he was moved to the Paraplegic Center in Pune for the remainder of his recovery.

As soon as he entered the center, he saw a figure rushing toward him and before he could react, he had been taken into a warm embrace. Seema and his family had been informed of all the events that had transpired at the war much later, and he had told them he would soon be moved to Pune. Seema had patiently been waiting for his arrival, and her patience was rewarded when she finally saw him.

She let go of him and met his gaze, and he could see immense pride flashing in her eyes. She tightly grasped his hand and whispered, "You've done your part for your country and for all of us. Now, it's our turn to do something for you." And thus, as Advay began his arduous journey of rehabilitation, Seema was his constant companion.

Shortly after, Advay's parents and Jyotika too arrived. Sridevi, her eyes brimming with tears, embraced him gently. "My brave boy," she whispered. Anand couldn't hide the pride and concern in his eyes. Advay saw his father come close to tears for the first time as he said, "We're here for you, son."

The presence of his loved ones brought a new energy to Advay's recovery. Seema was a constant source of support, helping with his exercises and encouraging him daily. His parents and Jyotika provided emotional strength, sharing laughter and stories to keep his spirits high.

With their unwavering support, Advay pushed through the long and challenging path of rehabilitation. He learned to walk with his artificial foot, and soon he was running, swimming, and performing all the activities he once enjoyed. His loved ones' encouragement and belief in him played a crucial role in his recovery, helping him regain his confidence and abilities.

When he started his journey, it would take him immense effort to even stand up straight. Within a few months however, he made tremendous progress. His grit, resolve, and mental strength to overcome his limitations were unlike anything the medical staff there had seen before.

Once, as he was out for a walk by himself, a feat that few others would have been able to achieve, the hospital staff admiringly told his family, "He is so strong-willed that it has inspired all of us too. We're sure he's going to make a complete and smooth recovery in no time at all!"

Anand, Sridevi, Seema, and Jyotika all exchanged a heartfelt smile. As Advay returned from the walk which he had successfully completed, he raised his arm and punched his wrist toward the sky in jubilation.

The wise warrior owl was ready to spread its wings and fly once again.

Chapter 13: Wings of Empowerment

Advay considered himself blessed to have made a good recovery. His progress was good, fueled by his own paramount mental strength, and aided by the unwavering support of his loved ones. Seema rarely left his side; she never let him feel incapable of doing things for himself and always encouraged him to be independent but at the same time, she had an almost magical quality of just being there whenever he needed her. Her presence was a constant source of motivation. She helped him with his exercises, cheered him up during his low moments, and celebrated each milestone of his recovery process with pure love and immense joy. His parents and Jyotika also provided emotional support, their love and care boosting his determination to regain his independence.

As Advay went through his recovery, he began to notice the stark and unfortunate difference between his own situation and that of many other patients at the center.

Seeing the loneliness in many people's eyes as they waited out their days there and tried to cope with their pain affected him the most. Unlike him, many did not have a strong support system. They faced their recovery largely alone, struggling not only with physical challenges but also the mental niggles that often accompanied such severe injuries. This realization stirred something deep within Advay. He saw himself in their struggles, but he also saw the difference that support and encouragement could make.

Whenever he could, Advay offered a helping hand. He assisted others with their exercises, shared motivational stories to help others strengthen their minds, and simply listened whenever anyone needed to talk. These interactions brought a new sense of purpose to his own recovery, as he found that helping others also helped him heal.

One evening, after his last physiotherapy session at the center, Advay sat alone in the garden and reflected upon his journey. The garden, over time, had become his favorite place to rejuvenate. He felt calm amongst the trees and flowers and it took his mind off his strenuous recovery. As he watched the sun set, casting a warm glow over the flowers and trees, he thought about the path that had brought him here, where it could have instead gone, and where he wanted it to lead next.

He softly smiled thinking about how, perhaps, if he had made different choices, he and Seema could have been enjoying their life abroad. Or, perhaps, he could today have been in a top-level executive position in some prestigious company within India.

But none of those experiences would have given him the same kind of contentment and fulfillment that his Army life had. He felt pride thinking about the sense of honor and duty that had made him join the Army, the camaraderie he had shared with his fellow soldiers, and the satisfaction of knowing he was protecting his country. He would not have traded that for anything in the world, and he held his experience of being an Army officer very close to his heart.

Now however, he was unsure about whether he wanted to return to that life, for he began hearing faint echoes stirring up within him of another call to duty.

It was a call to help those who, like him, had faced life-altering injuries but lacked the support to rebuild their lives.

Advay began to ponder the idea of dedicating himself to this new mission. He thought about the many soldiers he had met at the center, their stories of struggle and resilience, and the impact that even small acts of kindness had on their recovery. And he knew that there were countless others too, not belonging to the Forces, who would be grappling with such injuries and health complications. He felt a deep sense of empathy and responsibility towards them, realizing that his experiences had uniquely prepared him to understand and address their needs.

On the night before he was to return home, as he and Seema were talking about the future, Advay voiced his thoughts for the first time. "Seema, I've been thinking a lot lately. I have almost fully recovered now and I need to make a decision."

Seema had been very concerned to know about whether Advay planned to resume his Army service. She knew how passionate he was about the uniform that he wore and the responsibilities that came with it. While she dearly wished to never be separated from him again, she had been hesitant to stand in the way of his duty. She drew a sharp breath and fought to keep her emotions under control. She looked at him and evenly asked, "What do you mean, Advay?"

"I mean, I've played my part in the Army. I got a chance to serve the nation and I did it with everything that I had. I feel I have made a difference there. But now, I feel like I want to make a difference somewhere else. There are so many others who are going through what I did, and I want to help them. Being here has made me realize that a lot of people just need someone to support them, and that's what I want to do."

Seema gave a small smile, and admiration for Advay shined in her eyes. "You've always had a big heart, Advay. I think you'd be incredible at that. But are you sure? Leaving the Army is a big decision. I'm aware of how deeply you cherished it."

"I know," Advay replied, his voice steady. "But every time I see someone here struggling alone, I feel this desire to do something more. I've been blessed with so much support, love, and a strong mindset. I want to share that with others, to help them find hope and strength. I think there's nothing I would love to do more than that."

After making the decision to retire from the Army, Advay felt eager about how his future would unfold. He knew that making the switch from military to civilian life would feel very challenging at first, but he was ready for it. Memories of his time in the Army would always remain with him. Whatever he would do in life, he would always cherish the strong bonds formed with his fellow soldiers, the adrenaline he felt while fighting enemies, the satisfaction of completing missions, and the respect he had earned. They were a part of him, and they always would be.

When he finally reached home, his entire family gathered around to give him warm hugs. Sridevi's eyes sparkled with happiness upon seeing her son walk up to their doorstep.

"Beta, it's so good to have you home! I can make up for all the lost time now to fuss over you," she said, hugging him tightly.

Advay smiled, feeling the comfort of being surrounded by family. "It's good to be home, Maa. There's something important I need to discuss with you all."

They gathered in the living room, and Advay took a deep breath, feeling the weight of his decision.

"I've decided to retire from the Army," Advay began, looking at his parents. "I want to help others who have been injured like me. I want to do something to support them. You all were the reason that I'm back on my feet today, and I want to become that reason for other people."

His parents looked surprised, but also very proud of the man they had raised. Anand patted his son's hand and said, "We have always supported your decisions because we trust that you will always make the right ones. If this is what you now want to do, we will support you in every way we can," he said. His reassuring tone increased Advay's confidence in his decision.

Sridevi enthusiastically nodded and said, "It is such a great and noble idea! I never imagined it was possible, but you find some ways to make us prouder of you each day."

Before taking a step on the new path he had found for himself, Advay needed to take the last step on his previous path. He completed the retirement formalities from the Army and felt immense nostalgia and anticipation. While signing the final documents, his time there flashed before his eyes and he felt deeply thankful for having been given that chance. As he walked away, a new chapter in his life's glorious tale was waiting to be written.

He knew what he wanted to do, but the 'how' was still not clear. He wanted his work to be helpful for as many people as possible, and he dived deep into thinking and planning for how he could make it happen. But before he set out to make his plans into action, there was something he needed to do—something that had been on his mind for a long time.

One evening, Advay and Seema took a walk through the garden where they often spent time together. The setting sun cast a warm glow, creating the perfect, dreamy backdrop for what Advay was about to do.

"Seema, there's something I need to ask you," Advay began, stopping by their favorite bench.

Seema looked at him with a warm smile and asked, "What is it?"

Taking a deep breath, Advay reached into his pocket and pulled out a small velvet box. He beamed at her and said, "I would go down on one knee for this, but it's the doctor's instructions."

As Seema realized what was happening, she gave a yelp of happiness. Advay gently held her hand, looked lovingly into her eyes, and said, "Before starting with anything else, I want to take on the responsibility that is the most special to me- your responsibility. I have been away for far too long, and I don't want to spend another minute away from you. Will you marry me?"

She chuckled in delight and immediately said, "Yes!" It was among the happiest moments of Advay's life.

Their wedding was a beautiful celebration of love, surrounded by family and friends, including their wonderful group at college that had set the wheels of their beautiful story into motion.

As they walked around the sacred fire, Advay felt a unique and spiritual connection being made between them. It was a joy that he could not find the words for.

When the festivities eventually ended, and Advay found a quiet moment with Seema, he gazed lovingly at her. The realization that she was his partner in every sense warmed his heart. He felt a renewed sense of purpose and excitement for the future. With Seema by his side, he was ready to start his organization, dedicated to helping others rebuild their lives. Together, they would create a legacy of goodness, making a meaningful difference in the world.

Advay's goal for this next part of his life was crystal clear- he wanted to create a support system that would empower people to rebuild their lives and regain their independence.

In the living room of his home, Advay gathered a small group of fellow veterans to launch his remarkable initiative that he thought of naming, 'Wings of Empowerment.' For the wise warrior owl, it seemed the only befitting name for the establishment that he wanted to set up. He truly wanted to give them wings to fly high and reach new heights.

In the Wings of Empowerment, these wounded warriors would not only heal, but they would thrive. The organization became a safe place where challenges were turned into opportunities for growth with compassion and empathy.

Advay's vision for his organization went beyond helping in physical recovery. He imagined a complete transformation for the people who came to him; picking up the broken pieces of their spirit and making them stronger than ever. He aimed to help them learn new skills, find a new purpose, and rise above their disabilities. The veterans gathered at every session that Advay held, their eyes reflecting the shared pain and unbreakable spirit.

He thought meticulously about the goals of his organization-vocational training, counseling, and skill development. He wanted to teach others to navigate life differently, driven by resilience and courage. He wanted to replace every hesitancy that they felt with an inherent confidence. Advay's own transformation mirrored the ones he saw and brought about around him. His prosthetic leg, once a symbol of loss, now was a character of bravery. He encouraged others, through heartwarming stories, humor to lighten the soul, and constant support to see their limitations also with a new lens.

As word spread, more people arrived seeking help. Everyone came with a different struggle- physical, emotional, or both. Advay listened, shared, and became a shoulder for them to lean on. His sessions became a wonderful time for everyone to express their story and be inspired by the stories of others.

And so, Advay continued and surged ahead in his mission. He was the man who had turned his pain into purpose, and adversity into empowerment, and people truly believed that he would help them rebuild their lives. While Advay was delighted at the progress he had made toward his goal, he had no intentions of stopping there. He wanted to not only teach new skills to the people who came to him, but also ensure that they found a respectable livelihood.

He approached some of the best and largest companies in his city; he was set on opening those doors of opportunity for specially-abled people that had remained stubbornly shut so far. Advay relentlessly pursued the decision-makers in these companies. He had always been charismatic and persuasive, and his charm worked there too. He promised the companies a workforce that, like a diamond, had been formed under the toughest of pressures and which would shine bright.

On the first day of his trainees in their new job, Advay was extremely nervous. He paced the whole house restlessly, wondering whether the world would accept them.

"They will be just fine," Seema squeezed his hand and consoled him. "The combination of your efforts with them and their natural talent will make them unstoppable! You're worrying for no reason."

Advay tentatively smiled at her, hoping that her words would stand true. His very first trainees were a diverse group of talent. Among them were engineers, their minds filled with ideas for innovation; accountants, trying to solve numerical problems everywhere; and artists, looking for an outlet for their creativity.

Like Seema had predicted, the trainees were very well received and appreciated in their respective fields. Advay beamed with joy as he realized that the ways of the world have changed, and a person's ability mattered more than disability they may have.

Soon enough, many more people came to Advay in the hopes that he would work his magic upon them. They wanted to learn something new, or put their old passions and hobbies to a good use. They craved to have the chance at a respectable life, and nothing pleased Advay more than to be able to offer that to someone. He immersed his heart and soul into his work, and he thanked himself everyday that he had been given this chance to positively impact so many lives.

News about the Wings of Empowerment and the wonderful work being done by Advay and his team swept through the city like wildfire. Each new story that unfolded in front of his eyes and found a satisfactory end made Advay feel elated.

Jatin, a blind coder who had faced ridicule from society and rejection from employers, got connected with Advay. Recognizing his talent, Advay refined his skills and secured him a promising position at a reputable company. The coder did not need to use his eyes, for he was guided by intuition and sheer brilliance. He designed wonderful algorithms, and quickly proved to be an asset to his company. The CEO of the company, who had been rather difficult for Advay to convince, came to him within a month after Jatin's employment. "He is the most talented young man I have seen in my entire career. I cannot thank you enough for bringing him to me." Jatin gave a beaming smile at hearing the appreciation for his good work, and that smile reminded Advay of how many more such people he had to help.

Similarly, he helped Mrs. Geeta Chaudhri, a war widow, turn her life around. She was a woman who had been subjected to loss, grief, and uncertainty about where life would take her. But Advay helped her get it back on track. He saw the exceptional talent that she possessed in designing and stitching. With a mere few strokes of a pen and needle, she could envision beautiful clothes. He helped her fine-tune her talents, and within months, she was the right-hand person of a leading clothes boutique.

Mrs. Chaudhari came to his doorstep one day with a large package. When he asked her what it was, she urged him to open it and to his immense surprise, he saw that it was a wonderfully embroidered large owl soaring through the night sky. Below it, with equally fine embroidery, the name of their organization flashed. Advay held it close to his chest and profusely thanked her for it. She waved a hand and said, "You're the reason why me, and so many others, have found a new reason to live. Words can never be enough to thank you, and I hoped this would help instead!"

Advay excitedly hung it up in the small and cozy place that had become the office for his organization. And he looked at it every day, he felt a renewed sense of passion for his work.

Advay soon realized that it was not only individuals with disabilities who were seeking his help, and he had a chance to touch many more lives. Underprivileged and less educated people also began approaching him for employment opportunities. Advay saw this as an opportunity to expand his mission. He broadened the scope of his organization to include training and employment for anyone in need, regardless of their background.

As the years rolled by, Advay's organization underwent a remarkable transformation and blossomed into a full-fledged company that was successful, highly profitable, and driven by the ideals of goodness. From its humble beginnings in the living room of Advay and Seema's home, it now spanned across India. Advay was grateful to find like-minded and skilled people in other cities too who were equally committed to the cause and who helped set-up and manage the centers in other cities.

Pune, the birthplace of this movement, witnessed the first signs of progress. Here, young minds honed their skills and went beyond the boundaries of physical limitations. But the waves of growth did not stop there. They flowed to Mumbai, Delhi, Chennai, and many other cities. Advay frequently visited every other center to ensure that everything was running smoothly and that they were touching as many lives as they could with their good work.

With the expansion to new cities, Advay transformed his organization from a simple recruiting and training company into an exceptional institution. His innovative model of training and recruitment not only became a huge success but also set a new standard in the industry. Advay's organization grew at an unprecedented pace, rapidly extending its reach and influence. The expansion brought with it both success and prominence. Advay became a respected figure in the business community, celebrated for his dedication to social causes and his forward-thinking approach to recruitment and training.

As the company grew, Advay remained steadfast in his commitment to the core mission of helping those in need. Each new branch of his organization adhered to the same principles of personalized training and support, ensuring that every individual who sought their help received the assistance they needed. Advay's vision was not just about expansion but about maintaining the quality and integrity of the services provided. He ensured that every new branch was equipped with the best trainers, counselors, and support staff, all aligned with the mission of empowering individuals through skill development and personal growth.

The success of his organization brought financial prosperity, but Advay always remained humble and grounded. He viewed his wealth as a means to give back to the community in meaningful ways. Advay established numerous charitable initiatives, including scholarships for underprivileged students and academies that offered free training for those aspiring to join prestigious institutions like IIT, IIM, and the Armed Forces.

Advay's commitment to environmental protection was equally commendable. He contributed significantly to initiatives aimed at greening cities and rejuvenating lakes. His involvement was hands-on; he actively participated in and organized activities such as tree planting, river cleaning, and developing sustainable waste disposal mechanisms. Advay's efforts not only improved the environment but also raised awareness about the importance of respecting and preserving the environment.

The impact of Advay's work was phenomenal. He touched countless lives, offering hope and a path to a better future.

In every city where his organization established a presence, Advay fostered a sense of community and support. He personally visited each new branch, meeting with staff and participants, listening to their stories, and offering guidance. His presence was a source of inspiration, and his words of encouragement motivated everyone to strive for excellence. Advay's leadership style was characterized by empathy and a deep understanding of the challenges faced by those he aimed to help. He was not just a leader but a mentor and a friend to many.

Advay's influence extended much beyond his organization. He became a sought-after speaker at business conferences, educational institutions, and community events. He shared his insights on social entrepreneurship, the importance of inclusivity, and the power of perseverance. His speeches were filled with stories from his own life, showing how determination and compassion could drive meaningful change. Advay's message resonated with diverse audiences, from corporate executives to young students, inspiring them to contribute positively to society.

The financial success of his organization allowed Advay to expand his philanthropic efforts further. He established foundations that focused on various social issues, including education, healthcare, and environmental conservation. These foundations funded projects such as building schools in rural areas, providing medical care to underserved communities, and supporting research on sustainable technologies. Advay's approach to philanthropy was strategic and impactful, ensuring that resources were used effectively to create long-lasting benefits.

Advay's work in environmental conservation was particularly notable. He partnered with local governments, NGOs, and community groups to develop and implement sustainable practices. His projects included the creation of urban green spaces, the restoration of wetlands, and the promotion of renewable energy sources. Advay's efforts not only helped protect the environment but also improved the quality of life for countless individuals. Parks and green spaces provided recreational areas for families, while clean rivers and lakes supported local wildlife and improved public health.

Advay's dedication to social causes earned him numerous accolades and awards. He was recognized by national and international organizations for his contributions to social entrepreneurship and environmental conservation. Despite the recognition, Advay remained modest, always crediting his team and the communities he worked with for their support and collaboration. He believed that true success was measured not by accolades but by the positive impact one had on others' lives.

Through his unwavering commitment to helping those in need, Advay transformed not only his organization but also the lives of countless individuals. Advay's story inspired many to believe in their potential and strive for a better world. He showed that with determination, empathy, and a clear vision, one person could indeed make a significant difference.

Advay's transformative journey from the battlefield to social work was awe-inspiring. Like an owl watches over the twinkling night sky, Advay watched over those in need, guiding them towards a brighter future. The wise warrior owl had now become a symbol of kindness, empathy, and compassion. He continued to fly higher and higher, inspiring and helping many others to spread their wings and reach for the skies. His legacy of empowerment, compassion, and positive change would continue to inspire and guide future generations, ensuring that the seeds of hope he planted would grow and flourish for years to come.

VERSES KINDLER PUBLICATION

Verses Kindler Publication

Verses Kindler Publication

Reach us through our website -
https://www.verseskindlerpublication.com/
For more information visit our Instagram or Facebook page.